Sweet IMPERFECTIONS

Samantha Vitale

HEARTS UNLEASHED HOUSE PUBLISHING

For information about special discounts for bulk purchases contact:
hearts@heartsunleashed.com

Manufactured in the United States of America
Library of Congress Cataloging-in-Publication Data Vitale, Samantha.

Summary:

Sweet Imperfections follows the story of Katie Tayte, a young girl dedicated to her family and her best friend. It is a tale of two young women learning about themselves, growing up, and discovering what it means to sacrifice everything for the sake of another person. When an unexpected tragedy hits, Katie is faced with challenges that change the very fabric of her life. You will find yourself laughing, crying, and yearning for more with each page you turn in this amazing story about friendship, family, love, loss, hope, growth, and strength.

ISBN: 978-1-7376063-1-4

[1. Fiction. 2. Coming of Age. 3. Juvenile Fiction. 4. Girls and Women.]

DEDICATION

To my kids, I love you to the moon and back.

For Michael, it has always been you.

To my mom, for being awesome, loving, and ever supportive.

Last but not least, to my family and friends for your support and love.

Thank you!

CHAPTER 1

Where's Beth?

It had been two weeks since I'd seen Elizabeth Martin. She hadn't called, hadn't texted, hadn't sent a Facebook message, and hadn't been at school. I was really beginning to worry. Strike that…I was completely freaking out. Beth, formally known as Elizabeth and I had been friends since the third grade. We were practically sisters; joined at the hip, two peas in a pod…you get it! We had always been the best of friends. So, it was quite easy to imagine my freaking out about this.

"Dad! Can I please borrow the car?" I asked as soon as I got home from school. I was trying to make myself tear up. *Dad couldn't resist my sad brown eyes…could he?*

"What do you need the car for, Pumpkin?" Then he frowned, putting on his serious lawyer face. "Aren't you still grounded?"

I panicked. I'd gotten grounded for getting a D on my science paper last week. Surely, I couldn't still be grounded.

"Yes! She's still grounded!" yelled my annoying, seven-year-old little brother.

"You stay out of it, Paul!" I yelled back, hearing my voice crack. That got my dad's attention.

"Are you alright?" He put a hand on my shoulder.

"I'm fine. But… it's Beth." As I said her name I began to cry. Dad sighed and handed me the keys.

"You have two hours." I gave him a quick hug and kissed his cheek.

"Thanks, Dad!"

I practically flew to the Buick and threw myself in. Once I had the seat and mirrors adjusted to my liking, I buckled, rolled the window down, and backed out slowly.

As I got on the highway, I flipped on the radio. It would only take me about twenty minutes to get to Beth's, but I needed to calm down. Music had always been a mood stabilizer for me. I hummed a couple lines of one of my favorite songs by Nickelback and felt myself beginning to calm down, even if just a little. It was normal to worry about Beth. It wasn't usual for Beth to disappear though, not without saying something to me. We'd always been so close that we were more like sisters than best friends.

I pulled into the trailer park and stopped at number sixteen. It looked the way it always had, but I had a bad feeling crawling into the pit of my stomach as I cut the engine. I could hear the yelling—more like screaming. I slammed the car door and ran up the couple steps. I took a deep breath and pounded loudly. The door swung open and the smell of smoke and alcohol that drifted toward me made me want to throw up. I looked up and into Beth's stepdad's sweaty face. Clearing my throat, I tried to find my voice.

"I need to talk to Eliza..."

He slammed the door in my face before I could finish. I heard the screaming again and thought maybe I should just go, but then I heard her call out to me. It was the desperation in how she said my name that had me turning back around. This time I didn't knock. I threw open the door.

"Elizabeth!" I yelled.

Her stepdad started yelling at me, her mom Sheela and Beth came into the room. Elizabeth said a string of curse words I'd never heard before, and suddenly grabbed my hand. We ran to the car. It wasn't till I opened the door that I noticed she'd brought her backpack and she was beginning to cry hysterically.

I put the car into drive and waited for her to calm down before saying anything. It wasn't the first time she'd had to get out and stay with us for a few nights while things calmed down at her house, but this was different. I had never seen her so upset.

"Oh, shit! Shit! I'm sorry. Kate! I'm so sorry!" I shook my head, not really sure how to start.

"What's going on?" I finally asked.

"Just take me to your house." She continued to cry.

As I looked at her my worry tripled in size. Her wavy black hair was a terrible mess. Her usually bright, green eyes were puffy, red, and bloodshot. Her sun-kissed skin was pale, making the dusting of freckles across her nose stand out more than they ever had. Her cupid's bow lips that usually had a pretty, peach hue looked pale and cracked. Her nails were chewed off and her fingers were trembling.

We got to our house and I helped Beth put herself together before heading inside. My mom would freak if she saw her this way. As it was, I could hardly swallow past the lump in my throat. After she took a deep breath and put her tangled hair into a messy bun, I handed her my lip balm and she applied a good amount. With a smile and a nod, we headed inside.

My mom was, thankfully, in the kitchen making dinner, and my dad and brother, Paul, were watching sports. I put the keys in the bowl on the end table where we always kept them and led Beth into my room.

She put her shoes beside my boots in the closet, and I handed her a set of pajamas. She went to the hall bathroom and showered. We were nearly the same size so we shared clothes from time to time. She loved my soft, flannel pajamas the most, and I knew they would be comfortable for her to sleep in.

While she showered, I took a couple pillows from the guest bedroom and put them on my bed. Elizabeth always slept with three pillows, and when she slept over I was happy that I had a big bed. She tossed and turned a lot from nightmares. I grabbed an extra blanket from the hall closet and put it beside the two pillows. My room was done in lavender and blue tones, so I almost always felt calm and relaxed. My bedding was soft gray and white, so the bright yellows and red that I had grabbed didn't go with anything in my room. They were a comfort to Beth, though. She loved bold colors.

I put her bag in the closet next to her shoes and changed into my favorite navy blue sweats and camo t-shirt. I was putting my hair up when Beth came in.

"Thanks for the pjs and shower. I feel so much more human," she said.

I smiled, but didn't say anything. She used my brush to detangle her hair and noticed that she was avoiding my gaze.

"Can we talk later?" she asked. Her eyes were hopeful, and while I really wanted to find out what was happening, I shrugged.

"Whenever you're ready." She smiled and gave my cheek a quick peck.

"Dinner!" I heard Paul yell.

"Come on, let's go eat." I grabbed Beth's hand and pulled her along.

"Hi, sweetheart." My mom hugged both of us, and gave Beth a generous amount of lasagna and salad. I made myself a plate and brought the pitcher of tea to the table.

"Thank you, Anne," Beth said to my mom. Sometimes Beth called her 'Mrs. A,' or even 'Mom.'

"You're welcome, dear."

The conversations drifted from school, to work, to summer plans, until we were done eating. I offered to do the dishes afterward.

"That's alright. You and Beth have some catching up to do," Mom said. "Paul can help tonight."

I was thankful she didn't ask Beth any questions. I said my thanks and Beth and I headed back into the privacy of my room.

Wanting to talk, but still not wanting to pry, I turned on my small television and put on the Twilight movie because it was Beth's favorite. She squealed and threw herself on my bed. I laughed and joined her, bringing my knees to my chest, and putting my head back against my headboard. Toward the middle of the movie, Beth started to fall asleep, which was strange for a Friday night. We'd been known to stay up until two in the morning, talking. I realized she must have been exhausted. She looked as though she hadn't slept in days. I turned the movie off, and then the bedside lamp.

"Night, Kate," she whispered.

She was snoring before I could reply. I let myself relax into my bed and drifted to sleep.

CHAPTER 2

What?

The next morning, I woke to the sunlight streaming in my window. I noticed immediately that Beth wasn't in the room. The door was open and two of her pillows were on the floor. I stretched and walked down the hall. The bathroom door was shut, and the shower was running. I frowned, and walked quietly downstairs to use the bathroom. It was only seven-thirty in the morning. After, I climbed the stairs and waited in my room for Beth, snuggling back into the warmth of my bed. I was just beginning to doze off when I heard my door creak.

"Sorry," Beth said as she came in and closed my door. She still looked terrible. "Did I wake you up?" she asked, her voice sounding rough.

"Are you okay?" I asked, studying her eyes.

She nodded and sat down beside me.

"I feel like I can't get enough sleep lately, my body is drained."

"Are you getting the flu?" I scooted away from her a little. She smiled sadly and shook her head. "Maybe we should get you to a doctor?" I suggested.

"I went a couple of weeks ago." She still sounded strange.

My mind began to race. *A couple of weeks?* That was how long it had been since she had been to school, since I'd seen her. *How long was she planning to not talk to me about anything?* I needed answers.

"Does it have something to do with why you've been missing school?" I asked softly. She nodded, but didn't look at me directly.

"Alright, well I'm not gonna bug you about it, just know that I am here when you're ready to talk."

I climbed back out of bed and got a pair of jeans and a shirt from my dresser handing them to her. Then, I grabbed a pair of jeans and a shirt for myself.

"I think I'll go shower."

After barely a word from Beth I went to the bathroom and took a long, hot shower. I let the water beat against my back and washed my hair with my Moroccan oil shampoo and conditioner. I didn't get out of the shower until I began looking wrinkled. Then, I got dressed and went back to my room, only to find Beth asleep again. I placed my towel on my closet door, grabbed my brush, and left quietly downstairs for breakfast.

I could smell the bacon as soon as I entered the kitchen. My mom liked making big breakfasts on the weekends.

"Morning, Katie-Ann," she said without turning around.

How did she know it was me? I wondered to myself. I sat down at the island and she made me a cup of coffee. I closed my eyes as I took my first hot sip, felt it travel down my throat; smooth, creamy. If I had my way I'd drink more than one cup. Mom thought too much coffee was bad for you, though. I listened to the sizzle of the bacon and watched Mom make the French toast.

"Elizabeth okay?" she asked, handing me a plate of French toast, bacon, and eggs. I shrugged. She made herself a plate with smaller portions and sat beside me. "I know sometimes her home isn't… pleasant…" Mom continued.

I looked at her seriously.

"This is different, Mom. Something bad happened. I don't know what it was, but I just know it has to be awful. She isn't acting like herself. She looks sick, Mom."

My mom was frowning, as she often did when she was thinking about something. "I still think she needs to move in with her aunt. She'd be much better off."

"Yeah, but then I'd hardly see her!" her aunt lived in Oregon, and we were across the country in Stillwater, Oklahoma.

My mom busied herself with eating, so I kept my thoughts to myself while I finished breakfast.

"That smells amazing, Mrs. A." We turned to see Beth fully dressed with a smile on her face, the smile not quite reaching her eyes.

"Let's get you some breakfast." My mom rinsed her plate and grabbed a clean one from the cabinet.

"No bacon, please?" Beth asked. I looked at her inquiringly.

"I have to stay in shape for track," she reminded me with a shrug. She stuffed a huge bite of French toast in her mouth and moaned. "I could get used to this!" she said, her mouth still half full.

Mom and I laughed, and for the first time in the last two weeks, it felt normal. "You are welcome to stay as long as you need," Mom said to her seriously. My mom was the kindest person I knew.

"You girls want a spa day?" she offered suddenly.

Beth lit up instantly, making her green eyes dazzle. "That sounds so fun!"

"After we take Paul to Lance's house we will go."

As if on cue, Paul came into the kitchen and grabbed the plate mom had prepared for him.

"Where's Dad?" I asked. Usually, he beat us to breakfast.

"Oh, he had to leave early this morning. I tell you, I'll be happy when things calm down at the firm," Mom said.

Shortly after breakfast, we all pitched in with the chores. Beth helped do dishes while I swept the floor, and Paul took out the trash. None of us ever complained about helping out, we were used to it. Beth, of course, was told not to bother with helping, but insisted it was the least she could do for mom taking her in when she needed. My mom hugged her, and I couldn't help but notice the way Beth held onto her as if she hadn't been hugged in months. It made me feel so sad. *How could someone like Beth, who was so kind-hearted, have such terrible parents?*

"Well, I'll go get ready." I said after putting the broom back in the closet.

"Me too!" Beth said enthusiastically. Together, we did our hair and makeup. She'd always loved doing my makeup, so I let her.

"Green looks so good on you," she said as she put shimmery green eyeshadow on my eyelids. After we were done I put my flip-flops on and loaned her my other pair. Then, we all piled in my mom's van and headed out. I closed my eyes and basked in the sun.

"Here we are," my mom's voice interrupted my slumber. She walked Paul to his friend's door and waited until he was inside before getting back in the car.

"Let's go, girls!" Mom had said it like Shania Twain did in her famous song. We laughed, and after she turned on the radio, we were on our way. Once at the spa we all had a massage, then got our hair styled, and our nails and toes done. Beth looked like she was having a good time, which made both Mom and I happy.

After the spa, Mom treated us to some ice cream. Beth ate unusually little, and I ate too much. Then, Mom surprised us with a trip to the mall. She handed each of us fifty dollars and told me to text her when we were ready. We hugged her and thanked her profusely before making our way to our favorite clothing and music stores.

I got a new shirt and some earrings while Beth got herself a cute pair of yoga pants and a pretty top. She looked sad when paying and I gave her a comforting smile. I wasn't sure how comforting it was, but she smiled back. She wasn't used to being given money.

On the way back home we thanked Mom again, but did little talking. I figured we were all a little worn out from our trip. Beth's eyes began to close and she leaned her head against my shoulder. My mom smiled at me as she glanced our way.

"Looks like nap time." She spoke softly.

I nodded, feeling myself begin to doze off. It wasn't long before we were home though, and I looked forward to a little nap. It wasn't often that I felt this tired. I decided it was probably all the stress of worrying.

Beth lay on the couch and instantly fell asleep, and I told Mom I'd go lay down for at least an hour. Once in my room I shut the door and sat our bags down. Turning off the light, I set my phone alarm to wake me in exactly an hour, and fell blissfully to sleep.

It was one of those naps where you felt like you'd just fallen asleep when your alarm woke you up. I blinked and pushed snooze while I laid there and stretched. There was a tiny knock on my door and I knew it was Beth.

"Yeah" I said, and she came in. She looked as sad as ever walking toward me and I sat up, pleading with my eyes that she'd tell me something.

A small tear streamed down her cheek and I instantly grabbed her hand. My alarm went off again and I silenced it quickly.

"Beth, what is it? What happened?" She wiped angrily at a tear and sighed heavily.

"I'm pregnant."

I couldn't speak for a moment. I opened my mouth but nothing came out so I closed it again. Maybe I didn't hear her right. I tried again. This time all that came out was a squeaky "What?"

CHAPTER 3

The Beginnings of a Plan

Elizabeth told me as she sat down how she'd lost her virginity to a man she'd met at a bar. She had used a fake ID to get in. She cried and cried about how she'd been drunk and didn't know who the guy was. I sat and stared in both disbelief and horror. When she finally finished her story I didn't know if I was scared, sad, or angry. Maybe I was all three. I ran a hand through my hair and tried to take a calming breath.

"Beth," I started. I was on the verge of both crying and leaving the room. I took another breath. She didn't need me to be angry with her.

"We have to get you to the doctor." Beth shook her head.

"But, I already went." She said it in almost a whisper.

"I think my mom needs to know, and she will want to take you to the doctor." I tried to sound normal, but I sounded like I was being strangled.

"I know I messed up, Kate, but I hope you forgive me. I can't lose you." She began crying harder. I pulled her into my arms.

"You'll never lose me, no matter what." She nodded, but clung tightly.

There was a knock on my door and we both knew it was my mom. Beth's lower lip trembled, I knew she didn't want to tell her, but it had to be done.

"Now is as good a time as any." Beth didn't have time to react before I opened my door. My mom instantly pulled Beth into a hug. Then, she smoothed Beth's hair behind her ear and gave her complete and total attention. Beth began telling her all that she'd told me, and I felt as if I were having a reoccurring nightmare. When she finished, my mom looked as stunned and speechless as I had been. It didn't last long, however.

"We will set you up with an appointment with Dr. Ray; she's the best in the area." Beth nodded and wiped at her tears.

"Please don't hate me!" Beth blubbered, which put her in another warm embrace.

"Sweetheart, I'd never hate you. Elizabeth Marie Martin, you're like another daughter to me. Now quit your fussing, you'll make yourself sick. Go on and clean yourself up, we'll get everything worked out." With that she left the room, leaving Beth and me alone again.

"You're so lucky to have parents like that," Beth said as she wiped away the rest of her tears.

"We're always here for you, and if I had my way, you'd move in!" As I said the last part, I felt determined to make it happen. I didn't want her back in that hellhole she had to call 'home.'

I went downstairs after making sure Beth was alright. I found my mom on the phone, assuming she was getting the doctor appointment set up with her last OBGYN. Even as I thought about it, my mind swam. *Could this really be happening?* I grabbed a soda from the fridge and took a long drink. Then, I busied myself with a small tray of crackers, cheese, and broccoli with ranch. After a while, Beth came down and thanked me for making the snack tray. I laughed as she stuffed crackers in her mouth. My mom joined us in the snacking, and told Beth her appointment would be Monday morning. I felt disappointed that I'd be in school instead of with her. As if sensing my disappointment, Mom said she'd let the school know Beth and I would be late. When Elizabeth tried to protest, my mom shook her head.

"You're going to go to school, dear."

No one really argued with my mom. We finished our snacks in silence. It felt good to just let the quiet soothe my mind. So much was happening so quickly, I just wanted it all to slow down.

The next day we got up early for church, and although Beth didn't really want to go, she borrowed a skirt and wore the new top she'd bought. My mom braided her hair for her and again thanked her for deciding to go. Paul complained about having to go, but quieted after Mom reminded him he'd be able to go to the arcade in the mall if he behaved. We weren't bribing him to be good; it was more of a reward system.

We all got in the van and headed off. I didn't mind church, and admittedly enjoyed it because Bobby Farris was in my youth group, and I'd always had a crush on him. We were both a bit on the shy side. I'd been in school with him for a long time, and though he had friends, he was noticeably the quiet type. He'd even gone out with Mary Valerian, one of the popular girls. I'd heard it didn't work out because he wouldn't move past first or second base. So, I guess that meant that they didn't really make out or whatever.

My thoughts returned to the present when all of a sudden, Beth grabbed my hand and whispered "What if they ask where I've been?" She looked both scared and sad.

"You don't owe anyone answers," I said softly.

She nodded, but didn't let go of my hand. I didn't mind. I imagined I'd feel about the same in her shoes. Though, it was still difficult to imagine it at all. She didn't look pregnant, but she was different in some ways. Her face was pale, she looked tired all the time... but she was also more emotional than I'd ever seen her. Her eating habits and sleeping habits were changing. A big part of me hoped that she wasn't pregnant, but the other part was even more worried about how it had happened.

Dad parked the car and we all got out and went inside. Beth had let go of my hand but stayed close to me, my parents went toward the front, so Beth and I followed. Paul went to children's bible study down the hall.

Once we were seated, the pastor began. Beth fidgeted quite a bit at the start, but settled down after a few minutes. After we sang a few hymns and joined in prayer, our youth group met downstairs. Beth, of course, stayed with me. When asked to read part of the scripture she panicked so I read it for her, and I couldn't help but notice Bobby looking my way. I felt my face heat and hoped it wasn't noticeable. Beth however, noticed. She nudged me and giggled quietly, which turned my face to a flaming red.

After youth group, everyone broke into their separate crowds until church was over. Leanna, the group teacher, introduced herself to Beth and invited her to keep coming.

"Thank you. I'd like to," Beth replied, which surprised me.

"So, what's with you and Farris?" she asked once we were alone. I swatted her playfully.

"Nothing!"

She made a sound in her throat and suddenly said "Hi, Bobby." He smiled and waved in our direction, and to my horror, started coming toward us. *Balls!* There was no escaping.

"Hey, how are you?" he asked Beth.

She said something I didn't hear. I was too busy trying not to stare into his all-too-perfect gray-blue eyes.

"Hi, Katie," he said, turning to me.

I squeaked back a barely audible "Hello" before he was called away by his little sister. Beth laughed at me and I slapped my forehead.

"Why did you do that!?" I whined.

"You two obviously have a little something between you. Besides, you've liked him for years," she said quietly.

I didn't have time to reply before Paul told us it was time to go.

After church we went to the diner and had lunch. I picked the chicken finger meal with mashed potatoes. Beth got the cup of vegetable soup with a grilled chicken salad. Paul got a cheeseburger minus the onions, and my parents got the house salad. Once the drinks came I took a big swallow, the fizz from my soda tingling pleasantly in my throat on the way down. Beth had only asked for ice water, but she drank deeply and had to have a refill before we even got our lunch.

We talked about church and Beth told mom that she'd like to go again next week. My dad joined in on conversations at times, but when the food came we all ate in silence. Beth ate most of hers but asked for a box to take the salad home. Everyone else had finished. After the meal, we finally headed home.

Home at last, we spent the rest of the day relaxing before dinner. After eating, Beth and I took a walk, but didn't talk like usual. We got back to the house before dark. After the news, I went to bed. Beth had fallen asleep on the couch, so Mom had covered her and left her there. Once in bed it took some time to sleep, but when it came I slept like a rock.

I woke up with my alarm and hit the snooze twice before getting up. I grabbed my favorite pair of jeans, my new lavender t-shirt, clean panties and socks, then headed to the shower. Today was the day I would hear for myself what the doctor had to say about Beth. I washed quickly and got dressed. After brushing my hair I braided it and put it in a bun, placing my bobby pins in to hold it tight. I applied a little eyeliner and blush and glanced in the mirror. Satisfied, I grabbed my bag and headed downstairs.

"I like your hair like that." Beth greeted me at the stairs before heading toward my room to get ready.

"Thanks!" I replied cheerfully.

Once I was fully awake, I was usually a morning person. I made myself a bowl of oatmeal and Mom brought me a glass of milk. I ate and drank quickly, eager to get Beth's appointment over with.

Beth came down wearing one of my skirts and her black tank top with her hair in a simple ponytail. Mom and I both complimented her and she smiled but grabbed her stomach.

"Are you okay?" I asked, going to her side.

"I can't pee until we get to the doctor," she whined. I gave her a look of empathy.

"We'd better head out."

We got Paul out of the bathroom and took him to school. Mom called the high school and let them know Beth and I would be there a bit later.

Soon enough, we were at the hospital. Beth looked reluctant to get out of the car, but she did. It wasn't long after we sat that Beth's name was called and we were led to a small exam room. It was a bright yellow. *Meant to be cheery,* I assumed. We sat quietly while we waited. Beth looked nervous as she sat and fidgeted with her fingernails, or what was left of them.

A nurse came in and took Beth's vitals, then they stepped out to get her weight, which I heard her say was "one hundred and thirteen pounds." They came back to the room where Beth was handed a small cup. I could practically feel her excitement radiating from her. She was more than ready to use the bathroom.

Now I knew for sure, Beth was six weeks pregnant. Mom, Beth, and the doctor started "talking baby" after that, but I felt like I was under water. I didn't hear most of what was said. My mom stayed as calm as ever as the doctor talked to Beth about options and handed her pamphlets on parenting.

All the while, I sat feeling as if I were in a dream. After we left the doctor's office we got Beth's vitamins, and Mom drove us to school. Personally, I was grateful for the distraction. We headed to the office, and then went our separate ways until lunch.

School ended quickly, and soon, Mom came to get Beth and me.

"I'm going to keep it," Beth said softly after a few quiet minutes in the car.

"We need to get your things, and you're moving in with us until we get this all sorted out!" my mom said matter-of-factly. Then, we headed toward Beth's mobile home. Beth's eyes grew round with fright, and I held her hand. She wouldn't be going in alone.

As we got out of the van I kept hold of Beth's hand, and we followed behind my mom, who didn't seem to be worried at all. She pounded on the door but it went unanswered, so Beth used her key. We went directly to her room where we packed most of her belongings and stuffed them all in the van as quickly as possible. After a while, Beth began to smile.

"Thank you, Mom!" She hugged my mom tightly.

"I'll not be having you in this place in your condition. We'll go to court tomorrow and get you emancipated."

With that, we piled back into the van and left for home. Each exhausted, but feeling triumphant. *That had gone rather well, I couldn't imagine how it would have gone if her mom and step-dad had been there!*

CHAPTER 4

She's Definitely Pregnant!

I walked down the hall to the guest room, which had been converted into Beth's room. We painted the room in vibrant blues and greens and all her accents were red, black, and even bright orange. She'd picked the colors out of the color swaths Mom had given her to choose from. When it was finished and she had opened the door, she had absolutely loved it. She hadn't loved waiting to be able to see it; we wouldn't let her go in because of the paint fumes.

Beth was almost two months along now, and there was a slight roundness to her middle. *Only my family knew, for now.* We'd already gotten her emancipated and so far it seemed her mom didn't care. Her aunt did however know she was living with my family, and offered to take her in. Beth had thought it over as promised, but had told her aunt 'no.' I was relieved, I didn't know what I'd have done if she'd left.

I knocked on Beth's door, and when I stepped in I saw her sitting in front of her fan, eating crackers, eyes closed, looking sick. I walked over and rubbed her back.

"This morning sickness is pissing me off!" she said in her moody tone.

I didn't know what to say so I continued rubbing her back in little circles.

"Anne says to just eat some crackers, but every time I eat I feel like it just won't stay down."

"I'm sorry, can I get you some water?" She shrugged, so I headed downstairs.

"Beth's morning sickness isn't going away with crackers," I stated as I got a bottle of water from the fridge. My mom sighed and went into her medicine cabinet. She handed me a little bitty orange tablet. I looked at it. She quickly explained how they helped her through her pregnancy with me and Paul. Told me she kept them for whenever she gets motion sickness.

"Just have her chew the tablet and wait about ten minutes before she gets up to do anything." I shrugged, thanked her, and headed upstairs.

"Chew it," I told her, after she stared at it as I had.

She popped it in her mouth; I sat on her bed with her and waited for it to hopefully kick in.

"Oh my God!" Beth said loudly, making me jump. I assumed she felt better because she got up and started going downstairs.

"Mrs. A! I need more magic tablets!" She asked happily.

Mom laughed and got a new package of them out of her purse, and handed it to Beth. She told her to only take them when necessary.

"I'm glad I could help! Now who's hungry?" she asked. She pulled out her famous homemade breakfast pizza from the stove, half of it made with no bacon because it didn't agree with the baby. Beth and I both helped ourselves after it was sliced and ready.

"This is heaven!" Beth said after grabbing another slice from the half that was made just for her.

"Thank you, dear."

"Thank you for the half with no bacon. The smell is starting to not bother me as much, but I don't want to risk it." I wondered quietly to myself about how Apple-wood smoked bacon could smell bad.

"Well, when I was pregnant with Katie I couldn't really eat tomatoes. Tomato sauce, or even salsa. With Paul I could eat them, but I had terrible heartburn constantly." Mom said.

"I'll just be glad to be over this morning sickness!"

Mom and I both nodded. I grabbed another slice before Paul walked in and finished it off. For a seven year old, he could put away the food. I looked at the clock.

"I'd better get ready for work." Time seemed to fly by those days, and though I was happy school is out for the summer, and to have more hours at my job, the heat was already getting to me. I ran upstairs to shower and dressed quickly. After saying my goodbyes, I drove the Buick to work.

I got there with ten minutes to spare, so I stayed in my car for five minutes. As I headed in I said "Hi" to my bosses, Kellie and Sean. They were nice people, and I'd gone to school with their daughter Ellie until she'd graduated last year. I clocked in and immediately started working; making sure the cabinets were wiped down, cleaning the tables and booths, and putting some music on the old jukebox in the corner. I pressed a random combination and Elvis came on. I was just fixing a napkin holder when the bell dinged, signaling customers. I turned around and was surprised to see Bobby Farris smiling at me.

I took a quick breath to calm my sudden nerves, straightened my apron, and hoped my hair looked alright. He smiled wider as I approached.

"Just one today?" I asked.

He nodded, not saying anything. I sat him at the booth, got his soda, and handed him a menu. I was thankful that when I'd handed him the drink, I hadn't spilled it everywhere. Still, I wondered why my day had to begin like this. I walked back to the counter and waited while he looked over the menu.

When I went back to his table I felt more prepared.

"Ready?" I tried to sound confident, but instead I sounded squeaky and pathetic.

He smiled up at me, his eyes more grey than blue in the dim light. *Why'd he have to be so cute?* I wondered.

"I'll have the cheeseburger, no tomato though please?" He handed me the menu and my hand brushed his for a split second. My stomach flipped violently. I put his order in and was thankful when more customers came. By the time I had them seated, Bobby's food was finished and I took it to him.

"Thank you, Katie." He flashed me a white smile, making me blush, and I quickly tended to my other tables.

After Bobby paid and left I went to clean the table and put the $5.00 tip in my apron. I found a napkin on the seat and noticed it had something written on it. Curious, I read it.

Do you like me, Katie? There was a 'yes' and 'no' beside it. My mouth popped open, and I slipped the napkin in my apron while looking around to make sure no one was watching. This wasn't something that happened to me… ever. It had me smiling like an idiot for the rest of the day.

My eight hour shift went quickly and I headed home with a decent amount of tips for the day. My mom had dinner for me kept warm in the oven. While I ate I listened to Beth talk about her day and spoke little of mine, until it was bedtime. Beth squealed when I showed her the napkin Bobby had left.

"Ooh Katie! This is great!" She beamed.

I still felt happy, but another part of me was scared.

"You need to circle yes and hand him that napkin at youth group tomorrow." I shrugged.

"Oh come on Kate! You're seventeen. Go out already! You have been crushing on him for years!" I nodded, chewing on my lower lip.

"I've never been on a date, been kissed, none of it." I felt scared and unsure.

"Give it a shot, what could it hurt?" Beth said softly. I nodded.

"You're right. I need to go for it." Feeling slightly better I circled YES and put it with my Bible study notes.

"It's kinda cute, the whole note on a napkin thing." Beth smiled and I couldn't help but smile back.

It was cute, and Bobby Farris had always been the boy I had had my eye on. At least, once I became old enough to realize boys really didn't have cooties, and started being interested in them instead. I wasn't the typical girl. When I was in middle school I liked a couple of guys but was always more focused on class. It wasn't until almost 7th grade that I thought of Bobby as a hunk. I'd never been asked out or really flirted with. I'd been looked at, but that's as far as it had gone. Maybe because I was quiet, not popular, or the fact that I actually liked school. Whatever the reason, it seemed that something was changing. That night as I laid down, I closed my eyes and felt blissfully ready for that change.

The next morning, I woke and readied myself for church before coming downstairs. I was surprised to see Beth awake, ready, and eating a bowl of oatmeal. I made myself some toast explaining I wasn't quite hungry. My mom nodded, but I could tell she didn't like that I wasn't eating a good breakfast. After Dad and Paul finished with breakfast I busied myself with a few chores before we finally left for church.

I checked for the hundredth time that the YES napkin was still in my study notes, earning a few giggles from Beth. I put my finger to my lips, smiling. When we made it to church I was the first out of the car. Noticing Bobby, I sucked in a breath and headed toward him. I felt my face heat and held back the urge to turn back around. I quickly looked around to see if I was being watched, and handed him the napkin. Though, I kind of slipped it to him like I was on some spy mission or something. He gave me a quick smile before putting it in with his notes, and left before my parents caught up to me. Beth smiled knowingly, Mom acted a bit like she had seen, Dad hadn't paid any attention, and Paul had been talking to Lance. My mom patted my back as we headed to our seats.

Church went by quickly, and Bobby had a big smile on his face every time he looked my way. After youth, our family re-grouped together and were about to leave when Bobby came up to us.

"Hello, Mr. and Mrs. Tayte. I was wondering if I could take Katie to lunch today?" I felt my face turn a deep shade of red as my dad looked at me. My mom smiled kindly. "That is, if you would like to, of course." He was looking at me, expecting me to say something. I nodded, not really sure if I could talk.

"Why, I'm sure that would be fine if you'd like to go honey?" Mom said, looking at me. I was still in shock, but managed another nod. My parents said their goodbyes to everyone and Bobby promised to have me home right after lunch, which seemed to please them. Beth gave me a thumbs up before leaving with them. I followed Bobby to his red pickup truck. He opened the door for me and closed it before getting in and buckling up.

"The Club House okay?" he asked, his voice soft.

I smiled shyly. "Sounds good."

Neither of us said anything on the short trip to the Club House, which was just a little restaurant about a block from Sweeties. I'm glad he hadn't chosen my place of work to dine in. That would have been embarrassing, without a doubt. Once we got to the diner, Bobby opened the door for me again to let me out, and then opened the door for me at the restaurant. I had to admire his polite manners.

We got our iced teas and ordered two burgers with fries, then sat quietly for a moment.

"I'm really glad you came with me for lunch." He talked quickly and I couldn't help but wonder if he was as nervous as I was.

"Me too, thank you Bobby," I said softly.

"That note was stupid, huh?" he asked suddenly, and I couldn't help but laugh. "No! Not at all. I thought it was sweet," I admitted.

That had him smiling again. You'd think such a handsome boy like Bobby wouldn't be shy. It was actually refreshing to see.

"That's good. I was really nervous."

We both turned to see our food being brought to us. After a few minutes I couldn't help but ask.

"So, is this like a date?"

He looked at me with a fry hanging out of his mouth and I couldn't stop the laughter that bubbled out of me, he took it out and laughed along.

"Do you want it to be a date?" he asked, bringing my laughter to a halt. His voice brought butterflies to my stomach.

"I've actually never been on a date." I admitted softly. Unsure of how he'd react.

"Well, I'm happy to be your first date, Katie."

We both smiled and enjoyed our lunch date. I could hardly believe it was all real. As I closed my eyes by the end of the night, I fell asleep with a smile.

CHAPTER 5

Times are Changing

I was officially Bobby Farris's girlfriend, *EEEEK!* I had made a dent in my savings for the Jeep I wanted, and Elizabeth was going on four months pregnant with a more noticeable baby bump. Every day I touched her belly and did my best to keep her in happy spirits. It always made her smile when I greeted the growing baby inside of her.

It still scared me, but I felt better because she was here to stay and had all the love and help she needed. When I stopped to think about it, I realized that things were changing fast. I walked toward Beth's room and knocked softly until I heard her tell me to come in. She was laying down absentmindedly, rubbing her growing belly.

"I wonder if it's a girl or a boy," she said softly, with a goofy-happy expression. I sat beside her and placed my hand on her stomach.

"Boy or girl, it will be perfect." Tears welled up in her eyes and I held her hand. "I'm always going to be here for you." A lump formed in my throat, making it difficult to talk.

"You want to go out with me and Bobby?" I offered to cheer her mood, and she smiled widely.

"If Bobby doesn't care."

"He already mentioned that he'd be fine if you came along sometime."

After a few moments she finally agreed, making me feel even happier. She could've used some time out of the house.

Once I had helped Beth pick out something comfortable but cute to wear, I got dressed. I put on my favorite jeans and sky-blue talk top, and threw my hair up in a ponytail off my neck. The summer air was thick with humidity, and I didn't want to be a sweaty mess on a date with Bobby.

It wouldn't really be a date, since we'd be there with Beth. We'd just go to the movies and out for lunch. I'd already gotten permission from my mom. She and Dad really liked Bobby, and for that I was thankful.

After Beth finally came downstairs I gave her a wide smile, and we met Bobby in the driveway. After getting out to open the doors for us, he gave my hand a kiss and we headed out.

The theater was packed and we'd left early enough to try to avoid it. We waited in line and Bobby paid for the tickets. He got popcorn to share and we got drinks. Beth looked nervous. I'd already assured her that you couldn't tell that she had a baby bump in her outfit. Still, she worried and I suppose I'd have probably done the same. Bobby held my hand as we walked to a decent spot to sit.

They were showing *Casablanca*. I'd seen it before. Bobby kept hold of my hand unless he was taking a drink or passing the popcorn. We held hands almost all of the time, and although we hadn't kissed yet, a part of me wanted to. *What if I wasn't good at it?* I thought, as I glanced his way. He gave me a smile that sent my heart racing and I returned my attention to the movie.

After the movie, Beth asked if I'd be mad if she went back home. She had mentioned not feeling well—and I'd assured her I wouldn't be mad, and Bobby agreed to take her home before we went out to eat. I understood her not feeling up to it, but I felt disappointed. It just felt like she didn't really want to do anything anymore. I tried to not get upset by it, but I couldn't help the small part of me that missed our fun times. We still had fun, of course…it was just different now that she was pregnant. It wasn't like how it used to be between us. I felt my mood shift and tried desperately to cheer up after we dropped Beth off. Bobby didn't really know the situation, only that she was staying with my family. In some ways, I had been wanting to tell him.

When we got to the restaurant, he surprised me by ordering it 'to go.' I became very curious as he took us off the beaten path. He took the dirt road for a little while and we stopped. After getting our food, we walked hand in hand to a pretty little sitting park I'd never seen. The grass was plush and vivid green, and he sat in the wildflowers. I joined him with a surprised smile.

"I didn't know this place was here," I said, as I looked around the small spot.

"Well, I was driving around for the heck of it when I decided to see what was in this direction. I thought of you when I got here." His face reddened.

To change the subject, I handed him the fries and his burger and grabbed my club sandwich. We ate in silence, but it was peaceful and relaxing.

After we finished eating he put the trash in the bag and put it in the truck. I laid down, enjoying the soft blades of grass against my skin. I smiled when Bobby laid down beside me.

"I really love this," I said softly. He looked at me and my heart raced, as usual.

"Well, I'm glad you like it." He laughed slightly and I turned toward him. He laced his fingers through mine.

"I still can't believe you circled yes." His thumb was slowly tracing my hand, making my stomach flip-flop and my arms cover in goosebumps.

"I've always had a crush on you," I admitted to him quietly.

"Really?" he asked. *As if he hadn't known!*

"Yes, really."

He scooted closer to me and brushed a strand of hair off my cheek. *This was it!* I thought, as I slowly licked my lips. Then, he put his lips against mine. For a second, everything seemed to stand still, our lips were touching just barely, but my heart was racing so quickly. I ran a hand through his hair. Things began moving a little faster. Our lips were moving together in a magical way and my body was on fire. Suddenly, we pulled apart, gasping for air.

"Wow," he breathed.

"Wow," I echoed. We spent a little more time sitting and talking before he looked at the time.

"I better uh, get you back." I nodded, but didn't really want to go.

We walked to the truck slowly, as he didn't seem to want to go either. As I buckled my seat-belt he turned on some music and we headed back. When we got to my house I unbuckled but didn't move.

"Thank you for today." I didn't want it to end.

He smiled and rubbed my cheek with the back of his hand, then sighed loudly.

"Katie?"

"Yeah?"

He leaned over and kissed me.

"Goodnight," he said, after we broke off the kiss.

"Night."

Feeling light-headed and funny, I headed to the house. After saying "Hi" to my parents I went to my room and jumped on my bed. Beth came in with a curious expression.

"How was it?" she asked.

My face heated and I touched my lips as I smiled.

"He sure can kiss."

Beth squealed and leaped at me. We fell on the bed softly, laughing. At that moment I didn't think I'd ever been happier in my life.

"Well, it probably won't be as great as scoring a first kiss with a hot boyfriend, but would you like to go to the doctor with me tomorrow?" Beth asked, with one hand on her stomach. "I get to see the baby tomorrow," she added with a smile.

"Of course I want to go! I wouldn't miss it for the world." I rubbed her belly gently and she closed her eyes.

"Is it weird that that feels good?" she asked.

I said "no," and continued carefully rubbing her baby bump.

"I'm still getting used to it," I said carefully. She opened her eyes and I saw she was beginning to cry.

"Me too." Her lip trembled and I laid closer to her.

"You're not in this alone, Beth, no matter what." She nodded.

"Thank you." We laid there for a while until her stomach began to growl, and I laughed.

"I think it's dinner time."

We got up and headed downstairs. I could smell the fried chicken halfway down the stairs and we both inhaled deeply. I set the table while Beth grabbed glasses and the water pitcher. Then, I helped serve dinner. We all ate happily and talked about our day. I left out the part about my first kiss, but my mom gave me a knowing smile. *Maybe she could tell?* I wondered. She'd always known things before I could tell. I guess it's a 'Mom thing.' I ate another helping of the mashed potatoes and Beth had more chicken and corn.

After dinner I did the dishes and we all sat in the living room to watch "Wheel of Fortune" and the news before bed, though Dad had to carry Paul to bed because he fell asleep before the show was half over. Beth and I both went to our rooms right after the news. As I sank in bed I smiled as my mind replayed the day, and I fell into a deep and peaceful sleep.

The next morning, I sent Bobby a text to let him know I wouldn't be able to hang out, and after a few sad faces he wished me a good day. I sent him a kissy emoticon face and hopped in the shower. The day's plan was to go see the baby for the first time, and shop for the baby. I was nervous about both.

After my shower, I dressed in a pair of jean shorts and a t-shirt. It was already stuffy in my room so that meant that it was getting hot outside. I put my hair up in a messy bun and applied a little dab of perfume on my wrists. Then, I knocked on Beth's door just in case she wasn't awake. I found her going through her clothes.

"It's just so hot, I don't know what to wear!" She whined and I put a hand on her back.

"How about that summer dress?" I offered.

"Nope, it doesn't fit right." I twitched my lips and started helping her look. After twenty minutes, and a "breakfast!" from Paul, she settled on a cute pair of khaki shorts and a black shirt with a few red roses on it. She'd had it since the 7th grade. I put her hair in a long braid and we went downstairs.

"You girls look cute!" My mom complimented us as she pulled cinnamon buns from the oven.

We said "thank you" at about the same time, and I poured Mom, Paul, Beth, and myself a glass of milk. Dad was already at the office. We ate quickly so that we could take Paul over to Lance's before we headed to the hospital.

When the doctor was ready for her, Mom and I both squeezed Beth's hands and walked in together.

CHAPTER 6

Wow! There Really is a Baby in There

We stared at the monitor for what seemed like hours. To me, it felt scary, but it was also kind of beautiful. The sound of the rapid heartbeat was sort of captivating, and seeing the baby was a whole new kind of experience. I didn't realize I was crying until Beth held my hand and asked if I was okay. I nodded and wiped my cheeks.

"There really is a baby in there!" I said stupidly, and Mom and Beth both laughed. "Would you like to know the sex?" Dr. Ray asked.

Beth nodded happily as she rubbed her belly.

"Congratulations. It's a girl," she said proudly.

Beth's lower lip began to tremble and I felt like I was in a dream again. We left the office and headed for the mall after the appointment.

"Now that we know it's a girl, we can go shopping," Mom said cheerfully, as we entered Baby Land.

"I'm not due for another five months, Mrs. A!" Beth replied.

"Never hurts to get ideas, and you can pick out an outfit to put her in before she comes home. Her first baby blanket, first toy…"

My mom was excited, that much we could tell, and we also knew there was no stopping her. I walked around trying to be helpful but knew I was failing. *I didn't know how to do this,* I thought to myself. Beth picked up a pair of pink shoes and smiled.

"Look, how tiny!" She giggled with my mom.

I tried to join in, but felt left out and unsure what to do with myself. A soft, pink blanket with blue trim caught my eye, and I went over to feel the fabric. It was incredibly soft. I grabbed it and looked at the cover. It said it was plush microfiber, and 'Princess' was written in the middle. I held it out to Beth and she squealed.

"Her first blanket," she said.

This perked up my mood. I had actually found something and contributed to the baby shopping. I felt a little less useless.

Five bags later, we headed out for lunch. I didn't realize how hungry I was until I'd finished my entire sub sandwich before Mom or Beth were even half through their meal. I then slowly ate my chips while they finished.

"Next month we'll start getting more things, but not too many. I'd like to have a shower," Mom said quietly.

"Shower?" Beth and I asked. Then, I realized she meant a baby shower, and I smiled.

"That sounds fun," I added.

"I don't want a mess of people smothering me in gifts!" Beth exclaimed, looking on the edge of tears. My mom patted her leg.

"Don't you worry about it now. Eat your lunch so we can head home. I have to pick up Paul." She glanced at her watch which had me checking the time.

"I have to get ready for work soon too," I reminded them. I was covering Rebekah's evening shift from four to eight.

After heading home to change into my work shirt, I put my hair in a braided bun and headed off. I was early, but I didn't really mind. Better early than late any day.

My shift was busy and quick, just how I liked it. I'd wiped down my last table when the doorbell buzzer went off and I looked up to see Bobby smiling at me. I walked up to him, feeling that silly butterfly flutter in my stomach. He watched me walk toward him, making my face heat up.

"I thought I might've been able to catch you before you got off." He sat at the first booth while I clocked out.

Instead of going straight home, Bobby and I walked hand in hand around town for a few minutes.

"I thought about that kiss all day," he said as we walked toward the Buick.

"Me too." I felt my face flush as I admitted it.

He smiled and tucked a strand of hair behind my ear. Time seemed to stand still in moments like these. He moved closer to me and I lifted my eyes to his.

"Can I?" he asked. I nodded and we leaned against the Buick, our lips touching softly. It felt like magic, and my arms had a mind of their own as I brought us closer. I made a soft sound in my throat and he pulled away.

"Too much?" he asked.

To that I shook my head, and we kissed one more magical time before we said goodnight.

On my way home I drove slowly, my lips still tingling. Now that we had kissed a few times, all I could think about was kissing him. The more I thought about it, I wondered if he felt the same. I also had other feelings; my body's way of responding felt good, but it also felt strange and kind of scary.

I know kissing could lead to other things like love, lust, and sex. This had me thinking about Beth, and the fact that she was preg-nant. I sighed loudly as I pulled into the driveway.

When I got inside, my mom handed me a bowl of salad and a bottle of dressing. I didn't feel hungry, but knew I should eat. I let the family take my mind off of my thoughts and worries.

Beth woke me the next morning; I had heard something so I got up and found her crying in her room. I immediately went to her side.

"What's wrong?" I could hear the panic in my own voice. She wiped her eyes.

"Look at me!" she said angrily.

"I'm seventeen. I'm mooching off my best friend's family... I'm pregnant!" She blubbered.

"You're not mooching Beth, we took you in. Yes, you're seventeen, and yes, you are pregnant. But, we are in this together." I tried to cheer her up, but felt like a failure.

"We're not in it together!" she said suddenly. "You have no idea what I'm going through at all! Your life is perfect! Perfect boy-friend, perfect parents, and you're a freakin virgin!" She was prac-tically yelling.

I stood, shaking my head. A big part of me felt like yelling back. *How was her condition my fault?* I took a calming breath so I didn't blow up at her. I tried to tell myself that she was obviously having a bad morning.

"You are clearly upset, I get it. I'm going to go." I turned to leave, trying not to cry. I wrote a quick note for my mom on the dry erase board, got dressed, and jogged to the park.

I felt really angry. My family and I had done so much for her. We had been there for her through so much. When her mom was wasted, when her dad left, when her step-dad beat her!

I wiped the tears from my face. I knew that I couldn't relate to what she had been going through, but I wasn't perfect. I didn't choose the life I had. I knew I had a great family, but we had our problems, too! Nothing and no one is perfect, or ever could be. I sat on a bench and let the tears fall; it hurt to hold them in any longer. *Didn't she realize that this was hard on me, too?* I wondered. She was so harsh, when all I was trying to do was be supportive. *That was all I had ever done for her,* I thought. I hated feeling disrespected. I felt myself beginning to calm down enough to stop crying. I took some steady breaths, and then jogged a while more. The sound of birds and the feel of the wind on my face soothed me. Something about nature had always had that effect. Like music, it just put me in a better state of mind.

When I made it back home, Beth was sitting in the kitchen with my mom eating a grilled cheese sandwich. I grabbed a glass of water and chugged it, loving the way it cooled my throat on the way down.

"I'm gonna shower before lunch," I said softly. My mom nodded, but before I turned to leave, Beth stood.

"Hey, I'm really sorry about this morning. I know I said some pretty crappy things. I'm awful sorry Kate. Forgive me?" Her eyes bore into mine, pleading.

I never could stay mad at her for long, we both knew that. I walked toward her and gave her a quick hug.

"Of course, we all have our off days."

Seemingly satisfied, she sat back down to eat and I threw myself in a luke-warm shower. After I dressed I came downstairs, and made myself a PB&J sandwich, grabbing another glass of water.

Once we were alone in the kitchen, Beth sat close to me. She played with her hair in that 'I feel guilty' kind of way. I nudged her playfully with my shoulder, but she gave me a sad smile.

"I really do feel bad about this morning. I just felt angry, tired, hungry…" she paused.

"The hormones are normal," I said as I looked at her. I continued "Beth, I know things are different in so many ways. You're pregnant, so things are weird right now. It's something we've never gone through before. Just because so many things are changing, doesn't mean I love you any less. You've always been like a sister to me, you know that."

Her eyes glittered with new tears and she hugged me tightly. "I love you too, Kate." I rubbed her back.

"Ice cream?" With that, a real, genuine, Elisabeth-type smile lit up her face.

CHAPTER 7

Hormones, School, and Many Plastic Spoons!

I grabbed my new class schedule and grabbed Beth's as well. At almost five months along she was showing, without a doubt. She hadn't wanted to come to "meet the teacher" night with me so I went with Bobby. He proudly held my hand as we walked the halls together. *Who would have thought I'd have a high school sweetheart of my own? A little late, but better than never right?* Bobby smiled down at me.

"So, how is Elizabeth holding up?" he asked as we walked up to his truck.

He'd been pretty well speechless when she'd confided in our youth group and had told everyone there of her current situation. They had shown a lot of support, and for that my family and I were grateful. Beth had done a very brave thing and we were all proud of her. It did take quite a bit of convincing her that she wouldn't be able to hide the baby anymore. After a few crying fits, a pint of ice cream, and a few long glances in the mirror, she'd finally agreed it was time to just accept things as they were.

Bobby tapped my shoulder and I realized I hadn't answered his question.

"Oh sorry, she's doing okay, especially now that she isn't getting sick as much," I said as I buckled my seat-belt. He nodded.

"My sister had her baby a couple years ago, and she was really sick for the first few months. Then, she cried about everything," he explained as he drove me home slowly.

"Thank you for taking me along," I told him in the soft, nervous voice I used every time he looked at me with that smile; the smile he wore only for me.

He brought his lips to mine after he parked in front of my house. We broke off the kiss and turned after we heard a loud whistle and clapping. I rolled my eyes at Beth and laughed.

"See you tomorrow." I kissed his cheek and walked into the house.

I handed Beth her class schedule and placed a hand on her growing belly. My mom called my name from the kitchen.

"Yeah?" I asked cautiously as I entered the room.

"I want to talk to you about Bobby Farris." She said seriously. I started to panic.

"Now, I know he's your first boyfriend, and I'm not saying I want you to break it off or anything. But now that school is back up you need to be able to focus on your classes. This is your senior year..." She paused and waited. I let out a breath that I hadn't realized I'd been holding.

"I've always been a good student, I've only gotten that one D last year but that was because I didn't have a partner and had to do it myself, it was hard and I tried my best," I reminded her.

She nodded, chopping an onion. "I know, but I also know that a boyfriend can be distracting."

"I promise if it becomes an issue, I'll put my grades first." I assured her, though it did suck. I loved spending time with Bobby. Mom seemed okay with my answer so I went up to my room with my class schedule.

I laid on my stomach, thinking that it was crazy that I was already about to begin senior year, crazy that in a few weeks I would be eighteen. I looked over my class schedule again. English, followed by algebra, government, animal systems, and then it was lunch, Spanish, free period, and choir. Beth and I would be in Algebra, choir, and also have lunch together. I'd been hoping Beth and I would have more classes together. As if on cue, Beth knocked before entering my room to look at my schedule. I studied her face and nodded as she stuck her bottom lip out.

"Damn! I was hoping for more classes with you," she whined.

"Me too, this kind of sucks."

"I'm so nervous." She sat down with her hand protectively over her stomach. I sat up and hugged my knees.

"I know. That's another reason I wanted more classes together," I admitted. She gave a slight smile.

"Maybe I should drop out," she said suddenly. My eyes widened as I stared at her.

"Don't you dare! You've come so far, and it's senior year!"

She looked on the edge of tears so I gave her a hug and kept my head on her shoulder. "I'm here for you." I reminded her.

"Thanks."

I hoped that she wouldn't try dropping out. If it came to it I would have my mom talk to her. My mom definitely wouldn't allow her to drop out. She'd somehow convince her to stick with it if I weren't able to keep things smooth. Even in high school, people still acted like children. I know that's why she was scared, she didn't want to be picked on, or stared at. Some people just didn't know how to grow up.

"How about we have some ice cream and watch the Twilight saga?" I offered her after we'd been sitting silently.

Beth glanced at me with a smile that I hadn't seen in quite a long time.

"Really? No work? No Bobby?" she asked, her eyes wide and expressive.

"No work, no Bobby." I assured her. Bobby was babysitting his nephew, and I had the next couple days off. She clapped excitedly and got up to use the bathroom while I grabbed two small containers of strawberry ice cream and a couple of spoons. Then, I grabbed the movies after letting my mom know the plan. She thought it was a great idea and said she'd let me know when dinner was ready.

We got through the first three movies and my mom surprised us by bringing sandwiches and chips up for us. We ate as we watched the fourth film. It was funny that we had seen these movies so many times, but every time we watched them we still enjoyed them as much as the first time. During the final movie Beth fell asleep so I finished watching it and shut it off. I laid down carefully beside her and drew the covers up. She murmured something about the movie and I covered my mouth to keep from laughing out loud. I shook my head and rolled to my side. It took a while to fall asleep but after a while, sleep finally found me, though it was riddled with terrible dreams that woke me every couple of hours.

The next morning, I woke up feeling insanely tired and cranky. Beth must have gotten up because she wasn't in the room. I got up, drew the curtain closed, and threw myself back on the bed. By the time I woke and went downstairs I was surprised to see my mom and Beth cleaning the house tougher. My mom was vacuuming and Beth was folding laundry on the couch. I made myself a cup of coffee and didn't pitch in with the cleaning until my cup was empty and I had a bowl of cereal.

After the cleaning was finished my mom got Paul off the computer and grabbed the school supplies lists. We all piled in the car, Beth both complaining about going and thanking my mom for buying her the necessities she needed for school. I offered to buy my own to which Mom shook her head and told me to keep saving.

Once we made it to the store Mom shopped for Paul's supplies while Beth and I took a list and shopped for ours. We both got new backpacks. I got one with blue and purple paisley print on it, while Beth grabbed a navy blue one. Then, we got several packs of pens and paper, calculators, and binders. After my mom approved our things she had us both get new socks, shoes, and a new outfit for the first day.

"Mrs. A! This is too much." Beth's concern was, while nice, annoying at the same time. She knew that my mom wouldn't take 'no' for an answer. While at the store, Beth grabbed a few containers of ice cream and yogurt, and a bag of plastic spoons, to which Mom and I both laughed.

"You need to take it easy on the ice cream," My mom warned. Beth smirked.

"Baby loves it!"

I didn't have a response to that, so I continued trying on different shoes until I found a cute, but comfortable pair. Beth grabbed two pairs of yoga pants, and a couple loose fitting shirts. I went for a new pair of jeans, a skirt, and two tops.

Once Mom was happy with the shopping experience we went out to Massey's pizza. My mom got cheese sticks, I got wings, Paul picked a small pizza, and Beth got a salad along with one of Mom's cheese sticks.

We ate in silent contentment and my stomach was beyond full before I had a small slice of pizza that Paul wasn't going to finish. Still, I dipped it in ranch dressing and kept right on eating.

"Sheesh, someone was hungry!" Beth joked.

I gave a smile and took a long drink of my soda. It embarrassed us all when it made me belch loudly, except for Paul, who laughed and proclaimed it "Awesome!"

Once we were home I organized my school supplies and hung up my new clothes. Then, I grabbed my cell phone I'd forgotten to bring with me. I had one message.

Missing you. *How could something so simple stir up those crazy butterflies in the pit of my stomach?* I wondered. I quickly sent Bobby a text. **Sorry for not replying sooner. Was getting school supplies and forgot my phone. I miss you, too.**

Do you want to go out tonight? He was pretty quick getting back with me. I went downstairs with a hopeful smile. Beth was sitting at the table with my mom.

"Bobby wants to see me this evening. Is that okay?" I asked. They both looked at me at the same time.

"I suppose, but not for too long. We have the Slaters over for dinner tonight." Mom said unenthusiastically. The Slaters were Dad's co-workers, so the night would be full of boring conver sation.

"Okay." I nodded, not knowing why I had to endure it as well. I sent him another message, and about twenty minutes later we were hand in hand walking around the park.

"I was hoping to stay longer, but we have company tonight." I said it softly, but I could hear the irritation in my voice.

"It's okay. At least we got to see each other," he said, as he squeezed my hand.

We talked about our day, work, and upcoming school and before I knew it I had to go back home. Bobby kissed me a few times before we left the park and once more when he pulled up in front of my house.

"See you tomorrow?" his eyes melted me to a head nod before I got out and waved.

Once I got inside I grabbed a change of clothes. My nice black skirt, and a sparkly blue top I had chosen at the mall. I took a shower because I'd already started to sweat from the little walk around the park. When I was done, I got dressed and braided my hair to the side. After applying a little makeup I headed down-stairs to help my mom prepare for company. I smelled the grill and smiled. My dad was barbecuing ribs. I walked out with a platter for him to put the finished ribs on.

"Thanks, Pumpkin," he responded absentmindedly.

I went inside and helped Mom prepare the potato salad while Beth made a vegetable tray. My parents always made sure to have plenty of food to eat, especially when we had guests. Beth sighed and whispered in my ear that she didn't want to be around people she didn't know in her current condition. I couldn't blame her.

"Girls, I know this isn't ideal, but you will be respectful and stay at the table for dinner until they go to the den." My mom told us.

"Yes, Mom," we replied.

Paul walked in and pouted.

"I don't like the Slaters. They're boring!" he complained.

I contained my smile and chopped a green onion to put in the potato salad. My mom told him the same thing she'd told Beth and me. just moments before. Then, she helped get his bath started since he was sweaty, covered in dirt, and whatever else he had gotten into. By the time everything was set and ready, the doorbell rang. My dad welcomed them and I wasn't surprised to see their son, Kevin, with them. He was a snotty twelve year-old. I politely greeted them, as did Beth while she tried to hide her baby bump, unsuccessfully, I might add.

We got through dinner. I hadn't even been close to hungry because of how much I'd eaten at lunch. It was uncomfortable, especially for Beth. The Slaters hadn't said anything mean, but had stared a lot. Beth's emotions were sky high by the time they left. That night, she spent the night in my room after we talked for three hours straight. It felt like old times.

CHAPTER 8

We Are Seniors!

Beth and I entered our high school side by side. She was wearing a cute but loose-fitted blue top and yoga pants. She got several looks and there was a lot of whispering as we walked to her locker. I waited almost until the first bell before I went to class. I was feeling happy that no one had approached Beth, but a little sad that I hadn't seen Bobby.

I made it to my first class and was surprised by the fact that I didn't feel shy. I actually said "hi" to a few people and waved, or smiled back. *Maybe everything that had gone on had been a little helpful in a way,* I thought to myself. *Maybe this year would be a good one after all.* I did my best to focus on my assignment until the bell finally rang. Beth met me at my locker.

"I really don't want to be here," she said softly, looking heartbreakingly sad.

"Are you okay? Did something happen?" I worried that she'd mention dropping out again.

"The whispers, the stares, they're pissing me off!"

I didn't really have anything comforting to say, so I rubbed her back.

"Let's get to class." She shrugged, obviously not wanting to, but she followed me anyway. Bobby was with some friends as Beth and I passed.

"Hey there, beautiful." He kissed my cheek in front of everyone and left me blushing. At least it got Beth back to her smiling self.

"I'm glad my embarrassment amuses you," I said playfully.

"I don't know why you're embarrassed, it was so cute!" With that, we went to our math class. I was not too happy about the class itself, but at least I could be closer for support if and when she needed it.

The whispers began almost instantly, and Beth's sad expression fueled my anger. She glanced at me and back down at her desk. I glared around the room, thankful when Mr. Lanthy brought the attention off of Beth and to algebra. I did my best to focus. When math was over and the room mostly cleared, Beth came to my desk.

"See!" She started to stomp away.

I tugged gently at her arm.

"What?" Her bottom lip began to tremble.

"This will pass. Give it time. They will find something else to talk about within a few days at the least." I tried to sound hopeful, but in all honesty, I knew it sounded forced.

"Easy for you to say...you're not the one who's pregnant." Her voice broke as she turned to leave.

"Beth!" I tried to call out for her, but she was already headed to her next class.

Bobby caught up with me at my locker. He smiled, and as good as it felt to know that smile was for me, I still felt awful.

"Hey, what's wrong?" he pulled me toward him.

"People are rude. I don't know how to be there for her through this," I whispered. I felt his breath in my ear which, despite the fact that I was distracted, it still made me want to hold my breath to keep from trembling. He brought on feelings I had never experienced before.

"I'm here for you, and Beth." He kissed my cheek and went to class.

The rest of the day went quickly, but was still difficult. Bobby and I did our best to cheer Beth's mood at lunch and during free period. Later on in study hour, Bobby and I sat in the library and read together, holding hands when we knew the librarian wasn't watching. I'd been asked by several popular girls if it was true that we were dating, and I happily nodded.

"We've been going out since the start of summer." They'd seemed impressed. I honestly didn't care what they thought. I had other things to concern myself with.

After school, Bobby kissed me by the Buick as I waited for Beth. I was beginning to worry. She was normally quick to get out. I started walking toward the building when I saw she was talking to Garrett Stephens. Garret is a football jock with a nasty attitude. I ignored the fear and walked up to them.

"Just leave me alone, Garrett!" she was crying.

I pushed at him before I even knew what I was doing. He turned to look at me. I hadn't been able to push even close to hard enough, but I'd at least gotten his attention.

"Come on! Leave her alone!"

"What are you gonna do about it?" He moved toward me.

"What's going on out here?" Principle Turner had impeccable timing! Beth and I didn't need to say anything, he was looking at Garrett.

"Mr. Stephens! Why don't you come with me? You girls go on home." I took Beth's hand and we walked silently until we got to the car.

"Are you alright?" I put a hand gently on her stomach."

She wiped her eyes and blubbered something that sounded like "He's a jerk."

I took a calming breath before starting the car.

"Thank you, Katie. That was really kinda badass of you," Beth said with a smile forming on her lips. I let out a nervous laugh and nodded.

"I saw you and him, and before I knew it I was trying to push him."

"Dude probably weighs more than both of us together." We both laughed loudly at that.

"Yeah, I don't know what I was thinking. I just felt so scared for you." She stopped smiling and thanked me again as I pulled in the driveway. My mom was quick to welcome us both home and ask about our day, as she always did. Beth gave a sad, half smile.

"It was emotional," she admitted, and I had to agree.

"I'm sure things will get better in time, dear." Mom said, putting a comforting hand on her shoulder.

Mom turned to me. "Do you like your classes so far?" I nodded and told her about some of them. After a while, Mom busied herself with dinner and I took my book bag upstairs to my room. I didn't have homework. I changed into a pair of sweats and a t-shirt and threw myself on my bed, not realizing how exhausted I was until my head hit the soft, plump pillow. I yawned and closed my eyes for a little while. I knew I'd adjust to being back in school, I'd find the rhythm of it again. The emotional levels had been difficult and exhausting. I couldn't imagine how Beth was feeling. With that thought, I got up to check on her. Beth's bedroom door was cracked open slightly and I could see that she was lying down. I tapped on the door before walking in.

"Hey," I said, as I sat beside her.

"Hey," she replied, but kept her eyes closed.

I wasn't sure whether to leave her alone or just keep talking. I felt bad for her being alone so much, even though I knew she was used to it. Around here though, she needed to always know that there was someone to talk to and confide in. She didn't have to be alone.

"You okay?"

She shrugged her shoulders without opening her eyes.

"I'm just really tired."

"Well, I'm going to go downstairs. Would you like anything?" I offered. "No thanks."

I left as quietly as I'd come. When I got downstairs, Mom was making a salad to go with the spaghetti and garlic bread.

"That smells good," I said, grabbing a cup of water and gulping it down. "Need any help?" I offered. If I went back upstairs I figured I'd probably end up falling asleep. I started cutting tomatoes, celery, and cucumbers, and grabbed some fresh baby corn. We liked making salads full of different vegetables, it kept the salad from getting boring.

Once the salad was done I covered it and put it in the fridge while dinner finished cooking. Grabbing another cup of water I sat down, and my mom looked at me with her 'what's wrong' expression.

"Things were so emotional today. Beth had an awful day with everyone staring and whispering. I felt like a failure because I knew that I wouldn't be able to help. I don't know how to help." I talked quickly, feeling the frustration sort of start melting off of me.

"Sweetheart, you've always been an amazing friend to Elizabeth. All you can do is be there for her, for support. Even if you feel you aren't helping, Beth knows you are there for her. Sometimes, that's all a person needs, just knowing that someone is there." She patted my back and then gave me a hug. I felt a little better after confiding in my mom. She always had a way of making things seem better, even if it was temporary.

I helped my mom finish dinner and set the table as she welcomed Dad home. I got Beth up, and got Paul off of his game. Together we ate, and each talked about our day. Beth and I left out the emotional complications the day had brought.

After helping clean up, I sent Bobby a message. Before I went to sleep, I prayed that the next day would be a better one.

The next few days weren't as rough. As the week went by it got easier for Beth. She still hated it, but there was less whispering. After a full two weeks, it seemed things were okay again. I figured they must have run out of things to talk about, or had someone else to pick on.

It was Saturday morning when I woke to a tap on my door.

"Hmm?" I said, not awake enough to use an actual word. Beth walked in holding her stomach, as she usually does.

"Morning," I said, rubbing my eyes and sitting up so that she could sit. "Sorry to wake you." She sat carefully and then smiled. Her smile was contagious. "What's up?" I asked, smiling back at her.

"She moved."

I looked at her stomach with eyes wide. "When?"

"Just this morning. I was getting up to pee and I felt this strange fluttering and then, a kick!"

I placed my hand gently on Beth's stomach. I both saw and felt it. "Oh my God!" I squealed.

Beth laughed as tears flashed in her eyes, and I felt a lump swell in my throat. "That's amazing." I whispered. She nodded, her tears flowing freely.

"It's so overwhelming." She took a steady breath.

"It's beautiful." The baby kicked again, making us laugh loudly.

My mom entered the room with a soft tap on the door. Placing a tender hand on Beth's stomach.

"Have you thought of any names yet?" my mom asked, a small smile on her lips as she watched Beth's stomach jiggle.

Beth gazed at her, with a scared expression.

"Not yet."

CHAPTER 9

Naming the Baby

Beth stared at her stomach for what seemed like hours.

"You've got time to decide." I told her, trying to be helpful.

"Yeah, a whole three months!" She gave an exaggerated sigh and drew little circular motions with her fingers against her growing belly. She was getting big quickly, but she was glowing with a radiance I'd never seen.

"You could make a list," I suggested after a while. That seemed to perk her up.

"Yeah! I can write down all the names I like and we can look at it together." She got quiet and her smile grew wider as she thought of something else.

"Or, we can both make one," she said loudly.

I didn't know what to say. *Me? How would I know what name would be good for a baby?* As I looked at her hopeful face, I couldn't say no. I had to at least try to help. I gave a quick shrug.

Beth began writing down names almost immediately. I told her I'd work on mine a bit later because I had homework to do. She hadn't been too happy about it, but she'd accepted it as a valid excuse. I felt thankful, it would give me a bit of time to think of some names.

I worked through my homework trying to think about names, and helped my mom set the table for dinner. I started to mash the boiled potatoes, and then thought through a bowl of ice cream later at dessert. Finally, before bed, I told Beth I'd have a list by morning. She had pouted, but then agreed, saying it would give her time to think of more.

That night I did my best to think of names and was satisfied with what I had come up with. I sat the little list on my dresser and turned off the light.

Beth wasted no time handing me her list the next morning at breakfast. I sipped my orange juice and held it in my hand, reading them with a smile. I didn't want her to think I wasn't interested in helping her.

The list read:
Grace
Lilly
Sara
Maybelle
Ava
Christy
Theresa
Marie
Michelle
Maya Rose
Alice
Lexi

I scanned the rest of the list, there were over thirty names written down. My list didn't come close in comparison, and as I handed it to her I worried she wouldn't like it. She read the names one by one out loud, and tears glistened her eyes.

"Dakota, Daphne, Isabelle, Gracelynn, Star, Sabrina, Summer, Rayne, Libby, Lydia." She paused, taking a sip of water and a deep breath before continuing to read the names to me.

"Bella, Tabitha, Mae, Justice, Faith, Zoe."

I paused. " Look, Beth, No matter what name you decide on it will be beautiful and perfect."

After hearing the names out loud, I decided I hadn't done half bad. She set down the list and gave me a tear-filled hug. My mom walked in at that moment with a worried expression.

"Are you okay?" She rubbed Beth's shoulder.

"We are comparing baby names," I said, as Beth finally let go of me. My mom looked over both lists.

"These are really good." She said after setting them back in front of us.

"Yeah, I'm not sure how to pick one," Beth replied, taking both lists in her hand.

"Something will come to you," Mom assured her. While Beth pondered the list I decided to make cinnamon rolls for breakfast. They turned out to be just right, perfectly warm and fluffy. I ate from the middle out, enjoying every bite. We appreciated the slow and lazy Saturday until I went to work. After two hours of cleaning to kill time I was sent back home. Now that school was back in session, we had been a bit slower at work.

When I got home I was surprised to see Beth, Paul, Mom, and Dad making pizzas. I quickly changed out of my uniform, washed my hands, and joined in. I grabbed pizza sauce and slowly covered the little pizza I'd made with the dough left for me. Then, I covered that in a light layer of cheese before putting on a few mushrooms, olives, and some sliced red peppers. Then, I put my pizza in the oven next to Beth's all cheese mini pizza, and Paul's pepperoni. Mom and dad were still piling their large pizza with bacon bits, pepperoni, hamburger, cheese, and onion. I'd never liked a lot of toppings on my pizza.

The three of us watched our little pizzas cook while Mom and Dad put theirs on the rack under ours. Once the small pizzas were finished, I took them out and sliced Paul's for him before handing it to him on a plate. Beth bit into hers eagerly, cheese hanging to her chin. I laughed as I bit into mine, trying to match her eagerness and not pulling it off. Still, it felt like a special little moment; one of those small moments that I was learning to appreciate.

After dinner we all went our separate ways. Mom insisted the dishes were hers for the evening, Beth was back to staring at our lists of names for the baby, and Paul and Dad watched some sport show in the living room. I decided to go to my room and send a text to Bobby.

Hi, how was your day? I hope it was fun. I pressed send and waited. It wasn't a long wait.

Hey, gorgeous. It's been long, I had to babysit and work on my uncle's farm. How was yours? I miss you. I smiled widely and read it again before replying.

It was actually pretty good. We made homemade pizzas tonight. I miss you too.

Any chance you can see me for a little bit tonight? I glanced at the clock, it was only six-thirty.

BRB! I sent the message and literally jumped off my bed.

My mom was doing a crossword. She didn't need to ask what I wanted, apparently she knows my "Bobby face." She gave me a little smile and then thought about it.

"I suppose you can, but just try to be home by 8:30, okay? We have church tomorrow." I hugged her saying my thanks and reminded her that Bobby would be at church as well. I texted Bobby.

Pick me up?

Be there in about 10 minutes. I squealed and ran back upstairs to change back out of my pajama bottoms. I grabbed a pair of jeans and my purple and blue tie-dye shirt, and brushed my hair into a ponytail. After applying a little lip balm, I put my socks and shoes on, half running back down stairs. After saying a quick "see you soon." I walked outside catching my breath as he pulled up in front of the house. He got out and opened the door for me as always. As he got back in and began to drive, I couldn't help but glance at him. Even after dating over four months I still couldn't believe I was with him. He looked at me, then back at the road.

We ended up at the little clearing where we'd had our first kiss. My stomach flipped just thinking about it. He opened the door and held my hand as we walked toward the middle of the clearing. We talked about life; school, our family, our wants, and dreams. I told him about wanting to be a teacher, or a doctor. He told me about wanting to be a veterinarian, or a mechanic, or just run the family farm. I listened to him talk about how much he enjoyed working on the farm. I ran a hand through his hair and giggled.

"My cowboy." My cheeks instantly heated because I hadn't meant to say it out loud (and it had sounded so corny)! His smile widened and he brought his lips to mine, I felt like I could kiss him for hours. We talked and kissed, held hands, and laughed. It all went by too quickly and soon it was time to go back home.

"I hate having to take you home already," he said, wrapping his arms around my waist as I leaned against him. I could feel his breath against my neck.

"I don't want to go," I said softly. All was quiet as we sat there except for the singing crickets.

"I think I might love you, Katie." Bobby whispered. I felt my heart race, my eyes widened, my breath caught in my throat. He waited for a reply, but I was rendered speechless. *Did I love him? Did I even know?*

"Are you ok?" he asked after a while. I nodded.

"I think I might love you, too." I replied finally. My heart felt full as ever looking into his eyes. He brought his lips to mine, and I felt as though time stood still in that perfect moment.

I felt dazed as I went to my room and dressed for bed. After brushing my teeth I knocked on Beth's door. She smiled at me as I walked toward her and gave her stomach a kiss. I laughed as the baby kicked against my lips.

"She loves you," Beth said. Just when I felt my heart couldn't feel more full.

"I love her, too." I didn't realize I was crying until a tear hit my lips. I wiped my eyes and smiled.

"You okay?" she asked quietly. I nodded.

"It's just been a really good night."

She made me tell her what Bobby and I had done while we were out and she teared up when I told her what he said and how he'd said it. How that moment couldn't have been more perfect. After a moment of silence, she looked down at her belly and then back up at me.

"Gracelynn Michelle," she said, rubbing her belly with pride.

"It's beautiful, absolutely wonderful," I replied, putting my hand on hers.

CHAPTER 10

Love, Laughs, and an Unexpected Guest

Love… love…love… I played around with the word. *What does it mean to love someone?* To me, it meant time, patience, understanding, and respecting that person. Faith and trust. It meant pushing through the hard times, hand in hand. Being there for that person.

With Bobby, there were so many things I felt, all at once. New and exciting things. He made me feel nervous, dizzy, weak, and let's just face it… hormonal. Things I've obviously never felt before, things that challenged me.

I changed from my pjs to my long, black skirt and white shirt with lilies printed on it. I brushed my hair and piled it in a bun, holding it up in clips. I had noticed that being with Bobby boosted my self-esteem. I was beginning to think of myself as 'pretty.' I wondered if it said something bad about my character as I glanced in the mirror. I studied myself in the mirror, taking in my dirty blonde hair, lips that I always thought were too thin, my eyes that were always slightly too big on my small face. Then I stepped back and looked at my body. I wasn't too skinny, I had a nice waist and curves that I never really noticed.

Nah! There definitely wasn't anything wrong with feeling that you were blessed with a nice figure.

Pushing thoughts aside, I went downstairs for a small cup of coffee while everyone got dressed and ready for church. So far, Mom and Dad were both happy with my grades. I still didn't really understand why they would worry about too much time with Bobby. All in all I'm not the average teenager you'd see these days. I'm not into parties, alcohol, drugs, sex, or anything like that. I had never even been tempted to try.

I ate a bowl of cereal and finished my coffee while patiently waiting. I'd gotten ready a little early, but didn't mind waiting. It gave me time to fully wake up. I finished breakfast just as Paul and Beth got pop tarts open. My mom and dad had already had a small breakfast while we were still in bed. By the time everyone was ready, I was sitting outside enjoying the sunshine. We all got in the van and headed to church. Beth and Paul were giggling and I turned to see Paul's hand on her stomach. I couldn't help but smile at his expression.

"That's really cool!" he said loudly.

I could see her stomach move under his hand. It was cool…scary, but cool.

Once at church, we took our seats in our usual row and waited for service to begin. I smiled widely as Bobby walked in, looked at me, and winked. I gave a small wave before turning my attention to the book of hymns.

After church choir, prayer, and a few words, Beth and I joined our youth group in the room down the hall. We took turns reading scripture and said a prayer before breaking off into little groups to talk, and then it was time to go. Bobby held my hand and made small talk with Beth until she left for the bathroom.

"You're beautiful." He whispered closely, instantly turning my cheeks aflame, and my stomach aflutter. I thanked him, and turned to see my parents and Paul waiting.

"See you later," I told Bobby in a soft voice before leaving his side.

"Beth's in the restroom," I said.

"Well, I sure don't miss that part of pregnancy." My mom said with a laugh. My dad nodded in agreement. I decided to go check on Beth. When I entered the bathroom my shoulders slumped when I heard crying. "Elizabeth?" I called softly.

"In here." She was leaning against the wall.

I rushed toward her side, worried.

"Hey, what's wrong?"

"Nothing." She wiped at her tears.

"You don't cry for nothing." I said gently.

She gave a tired shrug.

"I'm just hungry, sore, lonely, tired all the time," she blubbered. I felt that useless feeling I got when I knew I couldn't help her.

"I'm sorry if I made you feel excluded or anything," I said, wondering if my being with Bobby was causing some of her problems.

"No! No, it's nothing to do with that." She wiped her eyes again before walking to the sink.

"I think it's just these stupid pregnancy hormones. I cry about everything these days," she said with a quick laugh. "I'll be fine. Can't be pregnant forever, right?" She washed and dried her face.

"Let's go eat," I said. I took her hand and we found the family waiting by the entrance.

"Everything alright dear?" Mom asked, putting a comforting hand on Beth's shoulder. I waved to Bobby who was standing by his parents. They all smiled and waved at me before heading out. We ended up stopping at the Clubhouse for lunch.

Being seven months pregnant, Beth's appetite was growing. She didn't have morning sickness anymore, but she craved weird things. Just the other morning she had wanted beef stew, it sounded like a disgusting thing to eat for breakfast. My mom had laughed and even went to the store to buy her some. She also always wanted something sweet, but we didn't always allow that. The baby was gaining more weight. So, to please my mom and to be careful she had a salad, some of my mashed potatoes, and a huge glass of water.

"You have an appointment tomorrow. We have to see how she is progressing." Mom said, patting Beth on the knee.

Beth smiled and rubbed her stomach, which was now much more large and round. She looked like she had a huge ball under her shirt, but somehow at the same time, she was glowingly beautiful.

School wasn't as much of a problem as it was before. She still got looked at, but now it was more curious than judgmental. A lot of the time she couldn't go anywhere without being asked how far along she was, if she was having a boy or a girl, and constantly being touched. Beth didn't seem to mind. In fact, it looked like she really loved the attention. It made sense thinking about it.

Beth had had a pretty lonely life. Besides me and my family, she really didn't have anyone else. Though she did keep in touch with her aunt through letters and text messages with the phone my mom had gotten her. I smiled, placing a protective hand on her stomach.

"I'll go with you." I told her, glancing at my mom for approval.

"I love you." Beth pulled me in a hug. I was adapting to her emotional outbursts. I hugged her back.

"I love you, and I'm here for you."

When we got home we were surprised to see someone sitting on the porch.

"Oh my God! It's my mom!" Beth looked white as a ghost holding her stomach defensively.

"You don't have to see her," I told her. Both of my parents agreed, my dad stating that since being emancipated she was under no obligation. Beth smiled a sad sort of smile, and I couldn't help feeling awful for her. I mean, the nerve of that woman, coming here after all this time! After everything she's done!

We all got out of the car, Beth asked us to go inside, and stressed that she was fine. We all listened but once inside I stayed right by the door. I felt guilty eavesdropping, but knowing the kind of person Sheela was, I couldn't just walk away.

"What are you doing here?" I heard Beth say.

"How could you up and leave that way?" Beth didn't get a chance to say anything. "You're my only child, and you just left! Got knocked up, and left. What the hell did I ever do to you?" she screamed. I felt my anger rise, and had to fight myself to stay put.

"What did you do to me?" Beth shrieked. "You were never there for me! You spent more time drinking, doing drugs, and getting laid than you ever thought about me!" I felt pride, happy that Beth was standing up for herself.

"Now listen here you little shit! You will come home and I will help you care for that little bastard you're having!" That did it, I was out the door. Sheela glared at me.

"This doesn't concern you!" She snarled.

"I beg your pardon, but it does. This is my property and that is my sister!" I snapped back.

"If I was your mother, I'd smack you right in your snotty little mouth!" She yelled in my face, I could smell the alcohol on her breath. Just then, my parents came out.

"You go on and leave now, and there won't be any trouble." My dad said, putting a hand on my shoulder. My mom held Beth tenderly in her arms. Sheela looked as though she wasn't going to cooperate, but thankfully she began to turn around and leave.

"Don't you dare come back around me! I will be a better mother than you ever thought of being!" Beth cried out.

I expected another outburst, but Sheela kept walking away, and didn't look back. I gave Beth a hug and looked into her eyes.

"Don't worry, we won't let her come near you or the baby." She nodded and took a huge breath.

"I'm so sorry for causing trouble for you all!" Beth wiped at her tears.

We brought her back inside, and my mom got out an ice cream and a plastic spoon. Beth laughed as she wiped her tears before grabbing the treat.

Things calmed down, and I felt overly happy for Beth living with us. How awful it really must have been for her living like that for so long. It made me wonder how no one had ever called the cops and gotten her out of there. We had been tempted several times but Beth had begged and pleaded for us not to. So, we hadn't. At least now I felt we were actually helping her. I wasn't sure what would happen when the baby came. Maybe Beth would stay until she was on her feet. Maybe she'd move to her aunt's. For now, she was where she belonged.

Bobby couldn't come over because he was babysitting, Beth wasn't in the mood to exercise, and Paul was at Lance's house. Mom and Dad were spending time together. I'd even called work to see if they needed any help. Unfortunately, they didn't. It was 7:00 pm on Sunday, and I was bored out of my mind. I decided to get ahead on some school assignments. Afterward, I sent Bobby a text goodnight, and later once I'd gotten an outfit picked out, I went to bed early.

CHAPTER 11

Winter Storms, Head Colds, and a Baby Shower

Winter blew in with a sudden urgency and we all bundled up, sitting at the table with hot cocoa. I sipped slowly, laughing as both Beth and Paul ate all the little marshmallows first. I always enjoyed letting the marshmallows melt to a creamy froth at the top.

Beth was eight months pregnant and waddling around feeling crappy most of the time. The once beautiful feeling of being kicked was now her daily complaint. How much it must have hurt her that the baby was playing drums on her bladder or jungle gym in her ribcage. Still, much as she complained, she smiled proudly.

School was canceled on account of the blizzard blowing in. Paul was excited until Mom told him he couldn't play outside until it stopped. He finished his cocoa and ran to his room to pout. Beth shuffled around in the new fuzzy pants I'd gotten her. They were Cookie Monster blue with bright yellow and pink stars.

I made another cup of cocoa for myself and spent most of the morning reading my book for English class. After that, we all sat together watching the news. From the looks of things, we were in for a long week. I always thought snow was beautiful, but not when it was blowing in from all directions as it was. I groaned. The rest of the day was spent watching the snow fall. Bobby called twice, which made my day a little better. He was pretty good at lifting my spirits.

The next day proved to be worse. I woke up coughing, sneezing, and had a fever. I refused to go anywhere near Beth, not wanting to risk her getting sick. As the day progressed however, she ended up sick as well. I felt bad for her, but Mom was quick to start taking care of us. She made homemade chicken noodle soup, had us drinking broth, as well as water, and juice. I got a message from Bobby before going to bed.

Get well soon love, text me when you can.

The next day, we were in the doctor's office to make sure it wasn't anything serious like pneumonia or the flu. We'd been told it was a head cold, which I had hoped. Beth and I both got prescriptions. Since Beth was pregnant they gave her something different than what they prescribed me. I couldn't even pronounce the name of the stuff. As long as it worked, I didn't really care.

After our prescriptions were filled Mom drove us home. She wouldn't let me take the car anywhere, she hated winter weather and didn't like me driving if there was any ice on the road. I reminded her I knew how to handle the weather and was capable, but as I've explained, we just didn't argue with Mom. Once home, I immediately took the medicine and went to bed after reading another message from Bobby.

Love and miss you.

I smiled and after reading it again, I replied. **I miss and love you, too. Taking medicine and heading to bed now.**

Good! Take care and get lots of sleep.

I didn't bother responding again, I put my phone down, and almost instantly fell asleep. I was a lightweight when it came to medication.

I woke up about two hours later to a knock on the door.

"Hmm?" I mumbled.

My mom came in with a cup of broth and a thermometer. She checked my temperature. It showed 99.9 degrees; it was slowly going down. I sneezed a few times before she handed me a tissue, then my broth and crackers.

I said "Thank you, Mom," but it sounded more like "Tank you, Bob." I sat up, sipped my broth, and ate the crackers slowly. I wasn't hungry, but I knew I'd be in for it if I didn't eat the little she'd given me. As I sat, I thought about how lucky I was for having parents that took care of us. I was thankful that Beth had us to take care of her.

As the day went on, my fever broke, and I could smell out of one nostril. It was wonderful! I hardly ever got sick, so when I did, I got hit pretty hard. I was grateful for the medicine I had received; it seemed to work quickly. I spent the rest of the day resting and trying to get better.

The next day, Beth and I both were nearly back to our normal selves, but Mom had gotten our assignments from school and kept us home another day just to be safe. So, we worked together studying and taking notes. We were both still a bit stuffed up, so we sounded funny.

Beth was sitting at the table having soup when Mom sat down and said "Let's plan a baby shower!" Beth looked thoroughly surprised, then hesitated. She had known Mom had wanted to plan one but still didn't really like the idea.

"I don't really know who to invite. I don't have many friends."

"Nonsense!" Mom huffed.

"We can invite some from church, oh it will be a great time, you'll see." Mom got out a notebook and started coming up with color schemes for decorations, and told Beth to just relax and leave the whole thing up to her. After a few moments of contemplating, she shrugged and finished her soup. She knew there wasn't a thing to be done once Mom had made up her mind.

As the week went by, we returned to school. I worked three to four days a week, and hung out with Bobby when I could. This was the last year I would attend school here, this was the first time I'd been in love. My best friend would be having a baby in a month! I silently wondered just how different things would be soon. *What would it be like?* I thought. I was realizing just how quickly time went by.

The final bell rang and shoved me out of my thoughts. The day had gone by quickly, and it was time to go home. I kissed Bobby before he left while I waited for Beth by the doors. She was walking slowly toward me, and when she reached me, I helped her down the stairs. I took my time getting home, knowing that Mom had a little surprise waiting for Beth. She'd whispered about it to me before I had left for school. She told me that she should be done with everything, but I wanted to give her as much time as possible.

My mom usually always went all out when she planned surprises like these. I remember one birthday when I came home and the whole house was decorated in an "Alice and Wonderland" theme. I had been through a huge phase that year, and had been so thrilled coming home and seeing it come to life.

When we got home, the house was decorated with pretty pink flowers, and pink and white balloons with pink and white ribbons attached to them. The balloons said "It's a girl!"

My mom shouted, "Surprise!" and Beth instantly began to cry, but with tears of happiness. The place was completely decked out. Mom must have had a very busy day getting everything put together.

"It's beautiful!" Beth said, wiping at her tears.

My mom took her bag, and I grabbed it to take with me upstairs. I put her bag beside her bed and then put mine on my desk chair. Then, headed down to see if there was anything I could do to help before the guests showed up. I ended up making two snack trays. One was filled with fruits and veggies, the other with cheese, crackers, and sliced ham, turkey, and salami. Beth helped herself to stealing snacks here and there while I tried to make the trays perfect. She'd laughed at me when I playfully whined that she was destroying my masterpieces.

My mom had sent Dad and Paul away for some father-son time while we held the baby shower. Apparently it was a 'No Boys' event. Before the party started, I ran upstairs to get the gift I'd bought and wrapped for Beth. It was a combination of mother and baby gifts. I'd found a large t-shirt that was white with pink text that said "It's a girl." I also got pink and purple baby socks, a little bright blue fleece hoodie, and a pacifier with a cute frog printed on it. In addition, I included a card, wrapping paper, bow, and a bag with cute rubber ducks to put it all in.

The guests arrived, mostly women from church. My boss came, and our youth group teacher. A couple of girls from school also came, probably because their parents had made them. Still, Beth was having a great time...not to mention the gifts. There were boxes of baby diapers, a couple of diaper bags, cards, and some even sent money. As Beth opened each present she hugged and thanked the person that got it for her. I smiled widely when she opened mine. She'd laughed at the shirt and smiled happily at the tiny socks, and I'd come to her for a hug so that she wouldn't have to get back up. She liked the exercise, but I didn't think getting up and down so frequently and quickly was really good for her and the baby. Besides, it was getting more difficult for her to get up.

It was great seeing how happy Beth was, and that she was actually enjoying herself. I'd known she hadn't really wanted a baby shower. She normally didn't really like being in crowds, and as big as she was, she really hated being around people in general. She often complained about taking up too much room, which was ridiculous. She wasn't fat, she was pregnant, and I had to remind her of the difference pretty constantly. She really did look good. Her skin was healthy, and her green eyes were vividly bright. Her smile reached them, making them seem even more green.

There were bottles, blankets, clothes, formula, pacifiers, a baby monitor, and a few clothes for Beth to wear during her final month. She'd made out like a bandit with the gifts, and had gotten over a hundred dollars in cash to be able to get more things as she needed, which of course had made her cry.

After the presents, we cleaned up the table and my mom brought out a cake and I helped by getting the paper plates and napkins. (Pink, everything was pink!) After eating the chocolate cake, some of the mothers told baby stories, some not so good. Some stories were about grueling hours of hard labor. Others, how often they were sick through their pregnancy, and how much they hated not being able to tie their shoes. Beth had loved those because she could relate to them. Some stories turned my stomach, like hearing how some of the dads ate the placenta after birth. *I mean, who the hell does that?* Yuck! My appetite was clearly lost.

Then, there were beautiful stories. Like when the baby would first open its eyes to look at the new world, and how sweet they smelled and how pink they were. Beth smiled as she cradled her stomach. She was radiant, and it was a beautiful moment. I took out my phone and took a picture of her. She wasn't looking at anyone, she wasn't aware of her photo being taken. It was a perfect moment.

After story time, we played games, and did a lot of talking. Beth had a wonderful time, and that was what mattered most.

"Thank you all for coming!" Beth hugged everyone. The party had lasted over four hours.

Once the guests left, I helped Beth to her room. My mom's gift was set up a little away from the bed, and all Beth could do was stare and cry. After a moment, she walked to the little bassinet and touched the powder soft blanket, and swooped up the little white stuffed bear. Beth then grabbed my mom in a hug.

"Thank you! For everything. You've always been like a mom to me. You've always been here for me. You've all done so much." She sobbed. It was hard to hold my own tears, so I just let them flow as well.

"Shh. It's alright dear. You deserve it all. We love you, and you belong with us." Mom soothed her.

I don't know how long they stood in that embrace; I let them share the moment as I snuck to my room to change. It had been a good, but very exhausting day.

I helped Mom pick up the presents and put them downstairs in the guest room closet. She wanted to get a nursery set up for Beth but wasn't sure exactly which room she wanted to do it in. She had two rooms to choose from: one that had just a few storage items to go through, and the other, which was a guest room that never really got used.

As I laid in bed later, I thought about what it would be like when Beth had the baby. *What would she look like? Would she be loud, like my brother had been?* He had always been a cry-baby. I'd been very happy when he'd finally learned to talk instead of crying for every-thing. I suppose it was only because he's my brother. I didn't know what would happen, but I knew Beth would be a really good mom. I grabbed my phone and sent a message to Bobby.

I missed you today, but it was a lot of fun. Beth had a great time at the baby shower. My mom really outdid herself. How has your day been?

He replied, **I'm glad she had a good time, and it sounds like** maybe you enjoyed it too. My day was okay, but lonely. I hate the days when I don't get to see you.

I smiled. **Awe! I'm sorry! I'll see you tomorrow though!**

Very true! I look forward to it. Are you in bed?

Yeah, snuggled in but not really tired so I thought I'd message you. Were you going to bed? I hope I didn't wake you.

Laying down, but not tired enough to sleep yet, he sent back.

I see. What's on your mind?

You!

I grinned again. It was nice to know that he thought of me seemingly as much as I thought of him. Being in love for the first time felt good.

What about me? I hit send and bit my fingernails, curious as to what he was thinking.

How amazing you are! That you are actually my girlfriend... you're beautiful, smart, and funny. I love the way you carry yourself... you are just an awesome person in general.

I blushed. **So are you.** I replied, then laughed when I saw what he had said.

You think I'm beautiful?

You're handsome! But also smart, funny, and I love spending time with you. I also love that you are so different from other guys. I mean.. you know? Like, you aren't a jerk. You've always seemed to be a sweet soul.

Thank you.

You're welcome.

We should probably try to get some sleep huh?

Yeah... I guess.

Okay... Well I hope you have a good night. I miss you.

You too. Goodnight.

I put my phone down, still not quite tired enough to sleep. So, I laid there in my warm bed, thinking about how good the day had been, and how good it felt to have such an amazing boyfriend.

CHAPTER 12

Braxton's "What's?"

"The doctor put Beth on bed rest due to some bleeding. She was also having...Braxton's somethings?" I glanced at my mom. She laughed.

"They're called Braxton hicks. They are false contractions. Most women go through them at this time.

"Oh," I replied as I looked at Beth. She looked miserable. I couldn't help but feel bad for her. It looked like painful business.

I brought Beth's homework home. She surprised me by saying she would rather be at school.

That was not something I thought I would ever hear her say.

"I just don't enjoy being catered to." She complained as I handed her assignments and a couple books to her.

"At least I won't fall behind!" she grumbled. I helped her study, and though she didn't want me "catering" to her, I did. She needed as much rest as possible. Beth was always used to taking care of herself, growing up in the way that she had. She'd had to learn early.

As I sat beside her, I remembered all the times she'd come to me. We had always confided in each other. I tried to be there for her, even though I couldn't relate to what she was going through. She sat up and started crying suddenly, and my mom rushed to her side in an instant. All I could do was stare stupidly, wondering what happened and how I could help. My mom had it under control, telling her to breathe and holding her hand throughout it. Her stomach looked extremely tight, and I silently wondered if the baby felt squished.

"How long do those things last?" I asked.

Beth lay back against the chair seemingly out of breath.

"Oh, they come and go," Mom replied for her, moving a strand of hair from Beth's forehead.

"So, what happens if they just keep happening?" I asked, hearing the panic in my own voice.

"I'm alright Kate, don't worry," Beth said as she sat back up.

I rolled my eyes.

"Don't worry? Beth, you're my best friend. I'm naturally going to worry. I'll try not to stress you out though. I'm sorry."

Beth put her hand on mine.

"I love you Kate, and I am blessed to have you in my life. Much as I don't like being catered to, it's nice to know I am cared about." I hugged her, and then got up to get her a glass of water.

I spent the rest of the afternoon with Beth. And that evening, bundled up before going to work. My dad took me and told me to just call when I was ready to be picked up. I nodded before running in. I took off my coat, hat, gloves, and scarf and put them in the break room. Then, I adjusted my shirt before clocking in.

"How's Elizabeth?" my boss asked.

"Hanging in there, she started having those little contractions though." My boss gave me a sympathetic look and went back to work.

I busied myself with cleaning before the dinner rush began. When it did we had more carry-out orders than anything, so after two hours I was sent home. I'd only made twenty dollars in tips, but it was better than nothing. I called my dad after clocking out, then bundled back up.

"Sorry we weren't busy enough, Katie!" my boss said before I headed out. I told her I understood, and when my dad pulled up I ran to the van and into the warmth. My dad had a worried expression that had me panicked before he even told me anything.

"We moved Beth to the guest room," he told me slowly. I waited.

"She just shouldn't be climbing the stairs anymore."

I breathed out a sigh of relief and smiled a little.

"I'm really scared, Dad. She just seems to be so fragile. I don't know how to help her." I felt tears fill my eyes and tried to blink them away.

My dad patted my arm.

"Princess, it's alright to worry. You're her best friend and she's in a delicate state, but don't ever feel like you aren't helping. You've stood by that girl for years. You're a wonderful friend. I know she appreciates you."

I nodded, wiping my face.

"Thanks, Dad." We spent the rest of the trip in silence, both lost in our own thoughts.

When we got inside I took my shoes off and headed upstairs to dress in my warm pajamas before eating a bowl of vegetable soup my mom had warmed up for me. I sipped it slowly, enjoying the way it warmed me from the inside out. Then, after thanking Mom, I rinsed out my bowl and checked on Beth. She was asleep, curled up on her side with her arm cradling her stomach. I smiled and gently closed the door, heading to my room to bed.

Since I'd just eaten I didn't go to sleep. I turned on the TV and watched a movie that was half over. I had no idea what was going on. It worked and made me tired. I turned the TV off and welcomed the bliss that a good night's sleep would bring.

I woke to the beep of my alarm and I smacked the snooze twice before I actually got up. When I went downstairs, Beth was up, dressed, and eating French toast and eggs.

"Surprised you're up already," I said sleepily as Mom handed me my plate.

"Doctor's appointment again." She grumbled, then started laughing.

"What's funny?" I asked, confused.

"Baby girl has the hiccups!" she replied, her face glowing with excitement. I watched in amazement when she pulled her shirt up and I could see the steady movement. I put my hand on her belly and felt a flip under my palm.

"She loves you," Beth said with a grin. I smiled back, she always told me that.

"And I love her, too." I kissed her belly and then turned my attention to breakfast before getting ready for school.

I dressed warmly, and took the Buick. The van was gone since my dad took the day off to go with Paul for father and son day at school. I drove carefully and parked beside Bobby. He was waiting for me in his truck. When I pulled up he jumped out and opened my door. He kissed me before I had the chance to move.

"Yummy. You taste like syrup."

I laughed as he kissed me again, then he held my hand as we walked into the warmth of the building. He walked me to my locker where he kissed my cheek before going toward his own locker. I could hear his friends laughing, but I didn't really care.

"Is Elizabeth okay?" I was surprised to see Lane Fields tap my shoulder.

I nodded. "She had to be put on bed-rest for a few days. She has a doctor's appointment today to find out how things are going."

She shrugged but looked at me with concern.

"Well, I hope she's alright."

"Thanks," I said before turning.

"Hey, Katie?" I turned back around.

"You're a really good friend." She walked away before I could come up with a reply.

Wow! A popular girl that actually cared! I thought. Then, I hurried to class before I was late.

I sat at lunch with Bobby until he had to go and was surprised to see Lane Fields sit down beside me. *What was I supposed to talk about? Should I stop eating?* I wondered.

"Hey," she said easily, as if it were perfectly normal for her to be sitting beside me. Her friends were all looking, but she didn't seem to notice or care.

"So, would it be okay if I came over?" she asked distantly. I raised an eyebrow.

"Look, I know I've always seemed like a bitch. I just want to talk to Elizabeth." I nodded.

"Here." She put her number on my hand.

"Text me or have her do it. 'Kay?" She seemed sad, in a way. It made me wonder what she wanted to talk with Beth about.

"Sure. See ya," I said before she walked out of the cafeteria.

It's silly, but for the remaining hours of school while I worked on my assignments, I silently pondered on what Lane wanted to talk to Beth about. After kissing Bobby, I went home and directly to Beth with her assignments, and Lane's number.

"What in the actual hell would she want to talk to me about?" Beth asked as I handed her the number I'd written down for her. I suppressed a giggle and sat down beside her.

"I don't know, but she was pretty insistent that you talk to her. She even asked if she could come over!" Beth's eyes widened.

"Hmm." She shrugged, grabbed her phone, and typed a quick message. I didn't want to be nosy, but I found myself wondering what they were talking about after a few sent messages. Deciding it wasn't my business, I went to the kitchen to help my mom finish dinner. After I put the broccoli and cauliflower in the boiling water and helped smother the chicken legs in Italian dressing, she already had the potatoes boiling for mashing. I washed my hands and went upstairs to do my homework. I knew that by the time I was finished, dinner would be done. I had over an hour of homework at least.

After dinner Beth went to bed not feeling well. My mom and I both checked on her, even Paul asked if she was okay. Dad came home from work late, and after cleaning up the dishes in the sink, I decided to go to bed as well.

Thoughts became dreams, and I tossed and turned through nightmares.

CHAPTER 13

The Secret

When Beth reached almost nine months she went to the doctor once a week. I felt bad for her, she was always tired. She had frequent company, some from youth group, who visited every week. Beth and Lane talked every day, and though I hated to admit it, I felt a little jealous of their newfound friendship. I didn't ask what they talked about, and Beth didn't tell me. Sometimes when Lane was over, I was invited to their conversations. I wouldn't tell Beth that most of the time I felt kind of like the third wheel... I never imagined either of us having something in common with Lane or any popular girl for that matter. Sure, Beth and I were pretty but we weren't the popular type. We never had the right personality for it.

I sat in the kitchen working on my English assignment listening to the laughter and whispers between Beth and Lane. Pretending to be uninterested, I kept my eyes on the paper in front of me. I'd always enjoyed my English classes, but I found that it was difficult to write. It is a creative writing assignment, easy, fun... Still, I sat with pen in hand and a blank sheet of paper. Feeling a bit defeated, I took my things upstairs, grabbed my phone, and flopped on my bed.

Hey, how is your day going? I hit send and waited for him to reply.

Hey gorgeous! I'm bored, rather be with you.

I'd rather be with you too! Can't focus on my creative writing paper. Kind of a first for me. I sighed as I waited for his response.

Haha, yeah. I'm working on Spanish, wanna trade?

LOL! No way! I'll figure out something to write.

I'm sure you will! How is Beth holding up? His question made me pause. Would it be childish to admit I felt left out? That I was scared about how much more things would change when she has the baby? Still, Bobby is easy to talk to. He'd probably understand.

Did you fall asleep on me?

I smiled. **Sorry, lost in thought. She's okay, but she hates being stuck in the house, with everyone catering to her. Seems to be enjoying Lane's company…it's kinda weird, them hanging out.** I took a deep breath and sent the message. It wasn't long before he replied.

I bet it really sucks. I can't imagine what she's going through… I know it probably feels weird that Lane Fields is there hanging out with her, but she does need the support. Maybe Lane is just trying to help? I don't know Katie, I guess it's normal to feel jealous or replaced. Just be patient with her. I'm sure she will come around.

I pondered his words; he always seemed to know the right things to say. Maybe he was right; Beth did need all the support she could get. Shouldn't I be happy that she had another friend to confide in?

You're right. She'll come around. I don't know how I'd react in her position. Thank you for being here for me.

Anytime, beautiful! I gotta finish this assignment up though.

I'll text you later, k?

Ok. Good luck.

I put my phone down and finally began to work on my assignment. Once I was finished, I figured it would get a B, at best. At one time, not long ago, that would have frustrated me. I've come to realize all one can really do is the best they can. I admit, I could probably do better, but with so much on my mind, it's hard to focus.

I put my assignment in my bag and grabbed my phone.

Just wanted to say goodnight. See you tomorrow. Xo's. I hit send and turned off the light.

I woke up the next morning feeling energetic. I got dressed for school, brushed and braided my hair, and half ran down the stairs. I came to a quick halt. Beth was on the floor, scrubbing at a spot. I put my hand out to her to help her up. She groaned but took the help.

"What are you doing?" I asked, looking for my mom.

"She went to get some eggs, I spilled the juice and wanted to clean it up." I didn't know whether to laugh or feel bad, so I did a little of both.

"Don't get down there like that, okay? Mom would understand and you can holler for me." I cupped my hand to my mouth in a playful demonstration. She finally smiled.

"Don't tell?" she pleaded. I nodded and helped her sit down, then poured her a glass of juice. She rubbed her stomach lovingly while she drank.

"Well, you only have just a couple of weeks left," I said sitting down beside her. She nodded, still cradling her stomach.

"I'm terrified, but happy," she said as she looked up at me.

I smiled back and poured myself a bowl of cereal. I offered her a bowl but she shook her head.

"Eggs," she reminded me. I remembered a time when Beth had hated eggs.

The next day at school I went to the restroom before third period. Just before I flushed I heard someone crying a couple of stalls away. I was torn between leaving her alone, or trying to see if there was any way I could help. I quickly flushed and began to wash my hands. There wasn't any more crying, but I could hear the sniffling.

"Go away!" she snapped behind the closed stall. I knew who it was. "Lane?" I asked softly.

She opened the stall and suddenly leaped at me. Hugging me and crying all over again. I patted her on the back, awkwardly.

"Hey, what's wrong?" I gently moved her hair off her neck. She mumbled and blubbered, but I didn't get anything she said. Once she settled down, I left her side long enough to dampen a paper towel and put it on her neck, then handed her some tissue.

"Thanks." She sniffed, and then she started apologizing.

"It's alright. I can catch up on whatever I missed," I told her. She shook her head.

"Thanks Katie. Look, I can't explain...not right now...not here. Talk to Beth. Tell her...tell her I said to tell you." With that, she left the bathroom in a rush, leaving me wondering what the hell was going on.

The rest of the day went by in a blur, and soon I was kissing Bobby before heading home.

"Young lady!" My mom stopped me before I could make it to Beth's room. She had her hand on her hip and was tapping her foot. Classic "Mom."

"Is this about missing a class?" I asked.

She stopped tapping her foot.

"I'm sorry for skipping a class, but there was some trouble with Lane. I just spent the period in the bathroom on the floor with her as she bawled her eyes out. She told me to talk to Beth." I explained. Mom took a minute to consider my explanation. To my relief, she didn't look upset with me anymore.

"Alright... But I want you to make it up to Mr. Fleming tomorrow," she said, I gave her a quick hug and went to Beth's room, shutting the door behind me. Beth sat up with more effort than usual, which took me from my original thoughts.

"You okay?" I asked.

She breathed heavily and smiled.

"Fine, what's up?" her breathing slowed back to normal and I sat beside her. "No need to move on my account," I told her as she tried to scoot over. She shrugged.

"Too late now."

"I need to talk to you. It's about Lane."

Her eyebrows shot up in interest.

"Okay."

"Well, she was crying in the girl's room. She wouldn't tell me what was wrong, but." I paused.

"But what?"

"She told me to tell you to tell me." It was a mouthful to say, and I felt uncomfortable, like I was intruding. It felt weird that Beth shared a secret with someone else.

"You don't have to tell me though." I said. Beth grabbed my hand.

"Katie… Lane is pregnant." I felt my eyes widen.

"She's five months along. I've been sort of helping her."

I nodded, not really sure what to say. Lane didn't even look pregnant. How could I have missed it? She had to have some kind of baby bump.

"I talked her out of an abortion," Beth said as she cradled her enormous belly. I didn't think she could get any bigger, but she had.

"Beth, I think you're amazing. You're so brave for doing this. You're going to be a good mom."

That evening, as I walked around the park with Bobby, many thoughts and feelings went through my mind. First I was still so excited to have such an amazing boyfriend. He was holding my hand while we walked. Second, I thought about how different things would be after the baby. Then, I thought how crazy it was that Lane was pregnant. I wanted to talk to Bobby about it. To confide in him, but I didn't want to risk anyone else knowing. So, as we walked we didn't talk much, both equally comfortable in the silence.

As the crickets began to sing we knew it was time for me to go home. Before we left the park, Bobby lifted my chin and gazed into my eyes. His eyes sparkled. As I smiled up at him, he brought his lips to mine with a kiss that seemed to touch my heart. I pulled him closer, wrapping my arms around his neck, and he made a soft noise in his throat that made my heart race and my knees weak. We broke the kiss and I let him hold me for just a little longer before he walked me home and gave me a small kiss goodnight.

As I lay in bed, I could still feel his lips on mine. I could still feel the wild butterflies in my stomach. *I'm in love with this feeling.*

CHAPTER 14

Is It Time Yet?

At the hospital, Beth held my hand tight as Dr. Ray examined her and the baby. She was relieved to hear things were going smoothly, regardless of the fact that she was two days overdue.

"I've been worried though, because she isn't moving much anymore." The doctor gave her a kind smile as we helped Beth sit up.

"That's normal. She is doing well, no need to worry. She is in the correct position. This is the stage where you are getting closer to delivery."

Beth nodded, cradling her heavy stomach.

"So, she's alright?"

Dr. Ray nodded.

"Would you like to hear her heartbeat?"

Beth began to glow with excitement. They strapped a funny monitor to her belly and the nurse and I helped Beth lay back down. Her belly a mountain compared to the rest of her small form. Then, we heard it. It was so fast, strong, but it was a beautiful sound.

Beth wiped the tear that escaped down her cheek, and I had to fight to keep my own emotions under control. *Was it stupid that I was crying too?* Beth looked over at me and smiled. I guessed maybe it was normal for me to cry too.

"I will see you in a week, unless that little girl comes sooner. Feel free to start taking a bit of a walk in the mornings. Exercise is good for getting things rolling." Dr. Ray said happily before we left the hospital.

"Well, at least I have permission to walk around again!" Beth said as I helped her in the Buick.

Most of the bad weather was over, and I couldn't wait for it to get warm again. I also couldn't wait for this evening, Bobby and I were going to go out to eat and catch a movie. Since my grades were as good as ever, Mom backed off enough to allow me to go out a little more.

Since it had been cold, we hadn't been busy enough at work to get many hours either, but I still always treated what few customers I got well enough to make decent tips. Since I hardly ever spent money, I had managed to save over two hundred dollars to add to my savings for the Jeep. My mom still warned me to hang onto every little bit for college. As I thought about it, I realized that in just a few more months, high school would be over!

Beth waddled to the house, with my help, and we sat in the kitchen together. Mom made us some hot cocoa and gave us each a fresh baked peanut butter cookie.

"How did the appointment go?" she asked. Since my little brother wasn't feeling well, Mom had stayed home. It was the first appointment she'd missed, and though she tried to look like it hadn't mattered, Beth and I both knew it had. I smiled and listened as Beth gushed on and on about the baby's progress and I joined in when she mentioned the heartbeat.

"It was beautiful." I said aloud, causing Beth's eyes to water, and my mom to smile.

"Don't you make me a grandma anytime soon!" she said jokingly. I spit out my cocoa and Beth snorted.

"Much as I'm excited for Beth, I plan to wait." We all sat and talked for a little while longer before we went on doing other things. Beth ended up taking a nap, Mom grabbed a book, and I got a message from Bobby.

Can't wait to see you, beautiful. The text read. No matter how often he called me beautiful, it still brought on that silly feeling.

Two more hours and I'm all yours! There was a pause, in which I flopped on my bed and waited for him to reply.

I hope you'll always be mine. I felt my stomach flutter.

For as long as you want to keep me. I replied, now biting my lip as my hormones kicked up a notch. He brought out so many emotions I was still not used to feeling. The way my stomach tickled, the way my heart sped. Most of all, the indescribable feeling I got just talking to him, and how he held me.

The time passed slowly, as it almost always did when I was excited about something. I applied a little makeup, smoothed out my sweater (more than once), touched up my hair; I'd curled it and put it in a ponytail. I paced around the house so much my mom told me I'd walk a hole in the floor. When his truck stopped in front of the house I actually squealed with excitement. Everyone laughed at me as I flew out the door.

At the restaurant, Bobby smiled at me from across the table, I was pretty sure my cheeks were as red as the napkin in my lap. We talked about school, work, and Beth.

"So, did the doctor say anything about her due date?" he asked, taking a drink of his Pepsi.

I shrugged, setting my glass down.

"Just that everything is looking good and that the baby is in the right spot. Her heartbeat is strong."

Bobby nodded and took another drink.

"You look really pretty tonight," he told me for the third time. I smiled and thanked him again. He always complimented me, but I hoped he knew he didn't have to so frequently. As much as I loved hearing it, I wondered if he said it because he didn't know what else to say.

"So, have you been filling out applications for college?" I asked.

He nodded and rolled his eyes as he explained the pressure his dad was putting him under.

"You get good grades, I'm sure you'll get into any school you choose," I reassured him.

Our food came out, and I was thankful. I took my plate of chicken fried steak and mashed potatoes, and he grabbed his BBQ sandwich with fries. We'd shared the side salad I'd gotten before dinner.

We didn't talk much while we ate, but both enjoyed the food. Before leaving the restaurant I offered again to chip in on the cost, and he frowned at me.

"I saved up for this, I've got it, beautiful." I blushed, and allowed him to pay, but I left a $20 tip on the table. He hadn't liked that either, but accepted it when I stuck my lip out in a pout.

We got to the little theater with twenty minutes to spare. I bought us both a drink before we found a quiet spot to sit alone. There, in the dark, the lights played against his face. His eyes were bright, and he seemed happy. We held hands and he kissed my cheek before moving toward my lips. I felt that familiar jump in my stomach. I giggled a bit, and he broke the kiss to find out why I'd laughed.

"You give me butterflies," I whispered.

He made a small sound in his throat before pulling me toward him again. My arms were around his neck, and my breath quickened.

We pulled away when the movie started, but he kept hold of my hand. I got up once to use the bathroom and freshen up, and after I sat back down he grabbed my hand as if his life depended on it.

After the movie, we took a little walk around the park. It was cold, but enjoyable. Then, he walked me to the door, gave me a quick kiss, and left before my dad came out to look at him funny, as he sometimes did. He'd told me that my boyfriends were supposed to be intimidated by him. I'd snorted at the "boyfriends" line.

Before going to bed I checked on Beth. She was already asleep with a book on parenting in her hand. I took the book and quietly set it on the nightstand, and turned off her lamp. I decided to sit in the kitchen to see how Mom was, and she was happy now that Paul was no longer sick. I headed to bed shortly after letting her know that my date went well, as it usually did. I, of course, left out the fact that Bobby had kissed me to the point of leaving me breathless.

In bed I re-lived the evening and wondered what the future would bring. *Would Bobby and I be together in college? What if he moved away? What if I did?* I let my mind wander as I knew it would. I was able to close my eyes and slip off to sleep sometime after midnight that night.

The next morning, I got ready for school before remembering that it was Saturday morning, which had everyone laughing. I laughed with them as I grabbed the cup of coffee my mom had made for me.

"Must have been one heck of a date!" Beth commented, bringing an instant blush to my face.

After breakfast I helped clean up. I did the dishes and laughed as I watched Beth dance with the broom. My mom put on some music and except Paul who had escaped to his room, we all cleaned and danced together.

Beth was so full of energy, dancing around with her beach ball of a belly and vacuuming the floor. I could hardly stop smiling.

That was before she stopped suddenly, and grabbed her stomach in a scream of pain. I threw the rag, running toward her. It seemed like I was running in slow motion, I just couldn't get to her quickly enough.

"Something's wrong," she gasped, before collapsing in my arms. We got her in the ambulance twenty minutes later, rushing to the hospital.

CHAPTER 15

Emotion Overload

In the waiting room I paced the floor, the smell of hospital making me sick to my stomach. *What was happening? Was she ok? Was the baby?* Thoughts continuously streamed through my mind and I bit my nails in agitation. My mom had dropped Paul off at his best friend's house, and even though it had been a quick stop, it had felt like forever as I sat in the van waiting.

An hour later, we were still waiting. My emotions continued to spiral out of control. My mom, though worried, did her best to stay calm. I could tell she was anxious by the way she tapped her foot as she flipped through magazines without really looking at them.

I finally sat down, crossing my arms.

"What is going on?" I asked out loud. My mom shook her head and put a hand on my arm.

"Try to stay calm, sweetheart."

I nodded, but didn't think it was possible. I took my phone out of my purse and messaged Lane. I just felt like she should know, that Beth would want me to tell her something.

Omg! Is she ok? She replied quickly, and when reading it I began to cry again.

I don't know, they haven't told us anything.

I'm on the way right now! I knew Beth needed the support she'd want Lane here, right? I messaged Bobby next, just to let him know. He'd replied that he was on the way as well. I felt a little better knowing that we had a pretty good support group.

Lane arrived and gave both my mom and I a hug before she began pacing as I'd been doing. Bobby arrived with two sacks of food and a drink carrier. I'd smiled at his thoughtfulness and ate for my mom's peace of mind, though I wasn't anywhere near hungry.

He held my hand and tried to strike up a conversation. I admired him for it, but I was at a loss for words. After about twenty minutes Lane started getting angry.

"This is ridiculous! We should have been told something by now." She flopped down on the chair beside me. I nodded, agreeing with her. She got up quickly and walked to the nurse's station.

"Yes, we have been waiting for a long time now for information on Elizabeth Martin, room 115. Her best friend is here! Can you see them waiting over there? Could we talk to someone, her doctor maybe?" The nurse apologized and to my surprise picked up the phone.

About five minutes after Lane sat back down a nurse arrived. We all stood, and held hands.

"She seems okay, but she's still asleep. The baby's heart rate has decreased, so we are keeping a close eye on her. We aren't sure yet what caused her collapse, but we will do everything we can to make sure that both mother and child are healthy and comfortable." We all nodded, happy to know at least something.

"I hope she'll be okay." Lane began to cry.

Unexpectedly, Lane threw herself in my arms. I held her awkwardly, but after a little while I began to cry with her. At that point Bobby rubbed my back, and Lane let me go so he could comfort me. This was the first time he'd seen me cry. He looked as sad and lost as I felt.

After nearly two and a half hours, Beth's Dr. came out to speak with us. I gripped Bobby's hand, fearing what she was going to say.

"She is okay, she's extremely dehydrated which is what caused her to collapse. We are going to keep her overnight for observation, but as long as she and the baby are fine, she will get to go back home tomorrow afternoon. You just go home and relax." While I was relieved to hear she was ok, I was also still upset.

"Why didn't anyone tell us anything?" I asked. The Dr. apologized and said they had been understaffed and overly busy. I nodded, and glanced down the hall.

"Can I see her?" I almost begged. Sympathy crossed her face and she led me to Beth's room.

It was strange seeing her on the hospital bed attached to monitors and an IV. Her face was pale, her lips white, and dry.

"Hi." She croaked. She sounded weak, and it scared me.

"Hey." I held her hand. She opened her eyes a little and smiled before closing them again.

"Beth?"

"Hmm?"

"Everything will be okay." She squeezed my hand a little before drifting to sleep.

As we left the hospital I couldn't get over how terrible she'd looked. How weak she seemed, after being so full of energy just that morning. My mom patted my leg and I realized we were parked in the driveway.

"She will be okay," Mom tried to reassure me.

I nodded, doing my best to believe it. I knew that Beth was in good hands, and as we went inside I did all I could to stay positive.

I ended up making dinner that evening. I preheated the oven and soaked the chicken in butter and seasonings. I covered it and let it bake for two hours. In those two hours, I cleaned my room, straightened up Beth's room, wrote in my journal, checked my Facebook, texted Bobby and Lane, and started boiling water for mashed potatoes. Before the potatoes were ready, I opened two cans of asparagus, and warmed them up with some butter.

By the time dinner was done I was exhausted, but hungry. I was surprised when Bobby came over to eat dinner with us. I smiled and thanked my mom for inviting him.

Everyone enjoyed the meal, and Bobby complimented me several times. My dad and even Paul had seconds. Afterward I cleaned the table and put the dishes in the dishwasher. Then, after getting permission, Bobby and I took a little walk. We held hands as we walked, both lost in thought. The night chill left a sweet smell in the air and had a calming effect on my mind.

"You okay?" Bobby's voice broke into my thoughts.

"Yeah, I'm just worried. I'm glad you were there at the hospital." He nodded, holding my hand a little tighter.

"I hated seeing you cry," he said softly before stopping to pull me close. I held him with my head on his chest, enjoying his heat, and the safe feeling of his arms around me.

"Sorry you had to see it," I told him.

He lifted my chin with his finger and brushed his lips against mine. For the moment while he kissed me, I thought of nothing but how good it felt. He pulled away and ran a hand through his hair.

"What?" I asked.

His eyes seemed to grow dark as he pulled me in for another kiss. This time, his tongue slowly slid across my own. My body went electric, my heart raced, my hands gripped at him tighter, and I found it hard to catch my breath.

"I want more of you," he said.

My mind suddenly began working again and I pulled slightly away.

"Sometimes I do too," I admitted shyly. He laughed a little leaning in to kiss me again, but I put my hand on his chest to stop him.

"I want to wait." I rushed.

I explained that I wanted to move out, go to college, and experience more things in life before… sex. He was quiet as I explained, and a part of me wondered if I'd disappointed him.

"I'd never hurt you Katie, and I won't ever pressure you into something you don't want to do."

"I know." I replied softly.

Grabbing my hand, he walked me home.

At home in bed I replayed the day in my mind. The morning had been a wreck, the evening had gone decently. As I lay there I prayed for Beth's recovery, and I prayed for the baby. I wiped away new tears and did my best to get some sleep.

I skipped breakfast and church the next morning and headed to the hospital in the Buick. When I arrived on the right level I went to the nurse's station. Beth's doctor was the first to see me. To my relief, she said that Beth was improving. I entered the room to find her eating breakfast.

"Hey," she smiled. Her color had come back, and she seemed more like herself. She was still hooked up to the monitors and an IV. I could hear her heartbeat and the baby's on the monitor.

"Dr. Ray says the baby could arrive in just a few days. I was so scared of losing her, Katie, her heart rate dropped so fast."

I nodded, holding her hand.

"I'm scared, too." I didn't tell her that I'd been scared of losing her. I sat with her for a couple of hours until she fell asleep again. Before leaving, her doctor told me she'd probably be released that evening.

When I got home I let my mom know everything, and spent most of the day cleaning to keep my mind busy.

Just before we headed out, the phone rang and I answered it.

"Hello?"

"Hello, Katie? This is Dr. Ray…" there was a pause and I suddenly felt sick to my stomach; that feeling you get when you know something is wrong.

"Hi, Dr. Ray. We were just about ready to head up to the hospital to come get Beth. Is she okay?"

"Beth is in labor. Her water just broke." I practically threw the phone and ran out of the door.

CHAPTER 16

It's Time!

When Mom and I got to the hospital they had Beth walking slowly down the hall. I frowned and before I could ask, Mom told me that walking would help her and the baby. I nodded and when I reached Beth she panted, grabbing for me.

"Make it stop!" she cried.

My throat felt thick and my eyes instantly filled with tears. I didn't know what to do. So, I let her lean against me as the nurse urged her to keep walking. Though she was sore, and tired, she stayed strong.

We must have walked for thirty minutes before the doctor had her laid back down to check her.

"Dang it. I'm sorry love, still only at four centimetres." Beth began to cry again, and my mom and I were immediately there to comfort her.

"We'll let you relax and try walking again in about half an hour."

Beth nodded, relieved that she could lie down. As the contraction hit, she squealed and held my hand so tight I thought she might break it. Before Beth walked again the nurse brought in some paperwork for her to fill out. She'd been happy to have an excuse to put off walking. My mom went to the cafeteria to get us a drink and some ice chips for Beth. She could have some water but preferred the ice. I stayed by her side, watching the monitor keep track of contractions, as well as her and the baby's heart rate. She filled out the forms and wrote the baby's name down so that they could get her birth certificate and social security card. After that, she was back to walking.

When we were alone she looked at me more seriously than ever. "Katie, promise me something?"

"Anything." I told her.

"If anything…goes wrong I want you and your family to keep Gracelynn." I stared at her wide-eyed.

"Are you serious?" I was almost speechless.

"Yes! You're my family." She told me, holding my hand for dear life.

"I promise, but Beth, you'll be fine! You've got this." I reassured her. She smiled a little half smile.

"Thanks Katie, I'm so scared, but I really want this baby out!" We both laughed at that.

As I watched another contraction hit, I felt helpless and rubbed her back with the hand that wasn't being squished. I tried saying calming things like "it's almost over, it will be okay," and "I'm here." Each time, she thanked me and we'd begin the slow walk. After a while she was able to lie down again, and to her frustration, be checked again.

"Well, you're at six centimeters, so that's good progress." The nurse said.

Beth smiled happily at the news.

"Soon, my sweet Gracelynn. I can hold you soon," she whispered.

After two more hours Beth was still only dilated to six centimeters, but was resting, so I took that time to go eat while Mom stayed with Beth. I grabbed a salad and a Sprite, taking a seat away from others. As I ate, I texted Lane and Bobby. Lane was sick and wouldn't come, Bobby was babysitting but said he'd come by after. I ate my salad quickly and finished my soda. After throwing away my trash, I headed back to the room.

Beth was awake, panting and breathing quickly when I entered.

"That was a big one!" Mom commented, rubbing a wet cloth against Beth's sweaty forehead. About as soon as the contraction ended, another followed. My mom frowned and pushed the call button for a nurse. Her doctor came in to check her.

"Okay honey, you're still not dilated enough to push. If it doesn't progress we will move you in for a C-section where I can get this baby out." Beth's eyes grew wide and she shook her head.

"No! No! I want it this way! Katie, don't let them take me!"

It was so hard to fight my tears, but she needed me strong.

"Beth, it's okay, alright? I'm not leaving your side. We're in this together. I've got you!"

She nodded, gasping when another contraction hit.

"Can you give her the enema or something?" I practically yelled.

My mom, the nurse, and even Beth laughed at me.

"I'm doing it naturally!" Beth told me through deep breaths.

"Are you nuts?" I gaped.

"Don't...make...me...laugh!"

I apologized.

"An enema is to help me poop!" Beth said after the contractions settled down, and I laughed so hard my ribs hurt.

"I don't know what it's called." I said, wiping the tears from my eyes.

"Epidural," she said, relaxing against the pillow. "I don't want any kind of medicine until after she's born," Beth said as she drifted off to sleep.

She wasn't asleep long before the doctor came in to wake her and check her progress. I held Beth's hand while she did her best to remain calm.

The doctor suddenly washed her hands and yelled for a nurse.

"What's happening?" Beth asked, but she looked awful. Sweat glistened her neck and face, and her lips were turning blue. Her eyes started flickering closed.

"Stay with us, Beth. You're bleeding, and we have to get the baby out now." A few nurses came in with another bed and lifted her up and onto it quickly. I could see a puddle of blood where she'd been laying and didn't even try to keep myself calm.

"What's going on?" I yelled, following the doctors. My mom grabbed me then and held me close.

"We can't do anything but pray now honey. Calm down, she'll be okay." She tried to soothe me, but her voice broke as she held me.

I was back to pacing the floor of the waiting room. I felt lost, powerless. I couldn't do anything and that fact pissed me off.

I got a message that Bobby was on the way, and suddenly felt like I didn't want to see him. I dismissed the thought nearly as quickly as it came. It wasn't his fault I was angry, confused, scared, and tired. I simply sent him a 'thanks' and left it at that.

When Bobby arrived he'd brought food with him again. This time, I didn't eat. I thanked him and told him I'd save the sandwich for later. He seemed to understand, and held tightly to my hand.

I got my hopes up a few times when a couple of nurses came out of the surgery room, but felt crushed when they didn't come toward us. I watched them run frantically to get things and rush back into the room. My heart was hammering in my chest.

About ten minutes later someone ran out of the room. I ran toward them, ignoring my mom telling me to wait. *I couldn't wait!* I needed to know what was going on.

"What's happening? Is she okay? Is the baby okay? Why won't anyone tell me anything?" I was yelling at the nurse, and crying again. She looked at me sadly and put a hand on my shoulder.

"We're really busy right now, sweetheart. I will send someone out soon." She tried to walk away but I shook my head.

"Please! What's wrong with my sister?" I put my head in my hands crying harder. She tugged at my hand so I'd look at her.

"She's lost a lot of blood. The baby got caught in the birth canal and we are working hard to keep them both alive." She let go of my hand, and she walked away, but I stood frozen in place.

"Keep them both alive." The words played over and over in my mind. I walked zombie-like back to my chair and both Mom and Bobby came to my side.

"I think they're dying!" I cried.

They both grabbed me in a hug. I cried so hard I felt sick. Bobby handed me a tissue. Then, he kissed my cheek and left, knowing I needed to be with my mom, and realizing there wasn't anything he could do, either.

Mom called Dad to let him know things were a mess and that we were just waiting. She asked about Paul, and when they hung up she was by my side holding my hand.

"I'm scared too, sweetheart." She cried with me. I didn't know how long we sat like that.

I began pacing the floor again while my mom went to the bathroom and to get us a bottle of water from the vending machine. I stayed close to the surgery room where they kept Beth. I heard her mumbling, I heard the doctor talking. Then I heard a baby cry. My heart skipped a beat and I felt a smile on my lips at the sound. My mom threw the water bottles and hugged me, hearing the baby for herself.

"She sounds healthy." She took turns laughing and crying. I nodded, happy but scared at the same time.

"I hope Beth is okay," I said. My mom grabbed the bottles and rinsed them off in the faucet.

When nearly thirty minutes passed and we heard frantic shouts and saw a nurse leave the room with a little bundle in her arms, my heart sped. Something was wrong, I could feel it. I stood and walked toward the surgery doors, hoping to hear Beth's voice. All I could hear was something about her heart, too much blood… I felt dizzy. The room was suddenly spinning.

"We're losing her!" I heard Dr. Ray shout through the commotion. Then, I felt myself falling. I heard a faraway scream, probably from my mom.

We're losing her.

We're losing her.

Everything was silent and I embraced the darkness.

CHAPTER 17

Living Nightmare

I shot up with a gasp, my heart pounding.

"What happened?" I asked.

"You fainted." Both my mom and a nurse I didn't recognize said at the same time.

"Where's Beth?" At my question my mom held my hand and the nurse excused herself from the room. My mom didn't talk. She stood there with her hand in mine.

"Mom! What happened? Is she okay?" Panic rose in my throat.

Mom began to cry. "She… oh, honey."

Now she was crying hard and I felt like I was going to throw up, or pass out again. I stood, pulling the blood pressure cuff off my arm and flinging it across the room.

"No! She's fine, she's okay...she's okay!" I screamed. I ran out of the room, running for the room they had Beth in for surgery. I felt like I was running so quickly, yet at the same time I felt like I wasn't getting anywhere. My chest hurt. I got to the door and I ran smack into Dr. Ray. She grabbed me to keep me from going in.

"Let me see her! I need to see her!" I screamed, not caring how loud I was or what I interrupted.

She held me as I continued wiggling around in her death grip. When I quieted I looked at her, pleading.

"Please! Let me see her. Let me see my sister."

She looked at my mom, as if asking permission. When Mom gave a little head nod she led me into the room. It was a little dark, it smelled weird, and it felt wrong. I walked forward, feeling like I was having some freak dream. She pulled the sheet enough to uncover Beth's face.

Pale.

Still.

Lifeless.

These words entered my mind. I touched her cheek.

"She's cold." I said softly. My mom rushed to me, and I fell apart in her arms.

"This isn't right… It's not fair! She was fine. She had been holding my hand…laughing." Through tears I looked at her face.

I don't remember how or when I got home. I remember my dad carrying me like a child to the couch. I didn't want to move, I drifted to sleep, thinking to myself it was all just a dream.

I watched through a haze as a plate of untouched food would come and go. Whispering from my brother as he looked at me. My mom, coming and going. I didn't care though, I just lay there, and all I could think about was her face.

Not being able to ignore my bladder I walked to the bathroom. As I washed my hands I glanced in the mirror. I didn't recognize the reflection of the ghost in front of me. I lay back down, on Beth's bed now. It still smelled like her strawberry shampoo. I grabbed her pillow and held it tight. *Would this nightmare end?*

The Funeral.

Saying goodbye wasn't my strong suit, and saying goodbye to the best friend I had ever had…I didn't know how to do that. There were people from school there, in the church. Some looked like they actually cared. Lane and Bobby were by my side. I was thankful for them to be there, but I didn't say anything. They didn't seem to mind. The pastor said kind words, and a couple of teachers spoke as well.

My mom and dad both said a little something, glancing at the casket. Closed, thankfully. I knew I should say something. I'd been trying to work myself up to do it. Mom and Dad sat down, Mom crying and Dad holding her, I stood and took their place beside the casket. I put my hand on the soft, cold surface, and fought through the pain in my throat.

"Elizabeth, so smart and funny; always there when I needed her. Elizabeth was my sister. She had very few friends, and very little in life, but she loved with all of her heart. She was my family." I paused and looked at my mom.

"Even though she's gone, she's in here." I held my hand to my heart, and choked on another sob. Turning back to her casket I lay my cheek against the cold, hard surface. "I love you! I miss you... I'll miss you every day, for the rest of my life."

Somehow, I got through the 'after thing' where people share food and say sorry. I don't remember much about it. Just that I didn't eat anything no matter how hard my mom tried to get me to. No matter how many people offered me food, I couldn't think of anything but her face.

Over the next week the school work began to pile up. I did it, my mind only half involved. I glanced at my phone and picked it up.

Are you ok? Sent at 8am Sunday.

Katie, please talk to me? Sent at 1pm Sunday.

Katie? Can I come see you? Sent at 10am Monday. I didn't feel up to company. I didn't feel up to anything, but I replied anyway.

I'm here, just need…time. Sorry. Sent to Bobby and Lane.

I ate when I had to, but didn't want to. After the week of being out of school, I told my mom I would try to go. When I got there I instantly wanted to leave. Everyone looked sorry for me. People were saying things like "hang in there," "are you okay?" "sorry for your loss," and "it gets easier."

I walked through the halls silently, not really acknowledging anyone. Bobby hugged me and held my hand when he could. During lunch I sat with him and Lane (who was bigger now).

"How is the baby?" Bobby asked sadly. I looked at him, frowning. I realized that I hadn't even seen her, or even thought about her. So, I looked at them both and shrugged.

"I don't know. Mom is bringing her home… today I think. I remember something about it anyway." Bobby nodded, but Lane suddenly stood crossing her arms, giving me her best bitch face.

"You don't know? She is your best friend's daughter! How do you not know? Have you even seen her?"

I fought back tears as I shook my head. People were staring.

"What the hell, Katie!"

"Hey! That's enough, alright." Bobby stood, and though I appreciated the fact that he was trying to stand up for me, I realized I was wrong. *Hadn't I promised Beth that I'd be there for the baby?* I put my head in my hands, unable now to stop the tears. Lane rubbed my back.

"I'm sorry Katie, but she was your best friend, and that child is the only thing that she left behind." I looked at her, and shook my head, standing.

"No, she left me, too!" I ran from the room, ignoring Bobby and Lane who were calling for me to come back.

I don't know why, but I was suddenly angry. *How could Beth give up? After all we'd been through, after all my family had done. Why did she leave us?*

I sat in the counselor's office. I didn't want to talk, but Principal Dixon had sent me when he found me crying and running through the halls.

"I know how hard this is for you," Mrs. Bradick said softly.

"I doubt it."

"Okay... if you don't want to talk, how about I give you a notebook to write in? Kind of like a journal of sorts."

I thought about it.

"Do you have to read it?" I wondered out loud.

"Not if you don't want me to. I think it may help you heal." I shrugged.

She handed me a blue notebook and a pencil. I don't know how long I sat there writing, but I didn't feel as angry and I was glad for it. I didn't want to be angry at Beth. I just... I just wanted everything to be as it was before she'd left. Before she'd gotten pregnant.

As I laid down in bed I heard commotion downstairs. I sighed and listened to it echo around the empty space. The baby must be here. I should have wanted to immediately see her, but I physically felt like I couldn't. *How could I? How could I not?* I felt the coming tears. Seems all I could do these days was cry.

My mom tapped on the door before coming in. As she came toward me, my eyes focused on the bundle of pink; it was the blanket I'd picked. I felt sick. I closed my eyes as she sat next to me.

"Katie..." Mom began. I shook my head, squeezing my eyes shut. She placed the baby in the cradle of my crossed legs, and I felt my heart break.

"Mom, please..." I cried.

I felt her hand on my shoulder.

"Honey, I know you're hurting, I know. But we're not the only ones she left behind." I sat there shaking my head, eyes still tightly closed.

"Open your eyes this instant! It's nobody's fault, you hear me? Now open your eyes!"

I clenched my teeth. *Damn it! I know she was right*, I thought. I couldn't blame the baby... Beth wouldn't ever forgive me for that.

I opened my eyes slowly, looking at my mom through a haze of tears. She nodded encouragingly. With a deep breath I looked down.

She was sleeping.

She was so small.

She had Beth's hair.

She looked peaceful.

She was absolutely beautiful!

The thoughts came to me in that order and I found that I couldn't look away. I heard my mom gasp, and pried my eyes from the sleeping baby.

"What?" I whispered.

"That's the first time I've seen you smile, in too long."

I touched a hand to my mouth. She was right. I looked back down. "Mom. Beth wanted…" my mom squeezed my hand.

"She's yours. I know. I know things will be hard. Beth wanted us to care for this little girl. Just in case anything…" She couldn't finish the sentence without crying.

"We'll figure it out…right?" I tried to sound positive, hopeful. Mom nodded. We looked at the sleeping baby.

"We'll help you care for her while you finish school, and as you go through college." Mom started. I blew out a deep breath.

"One step at a time," I whispered.

Mom offered to take the baby and I shook my head, I wasn't ready to let her go just yet. She went downstairs to make dinner. Now that I was alone, more emotions began to surface.

"You had the most amazing mom," I whispered, touching her soft little cheek with my finger. Her skin was so pretty, and unbelievably soft. "You have her hair," I continued quietly and watched her move a little in the blanket she was wrapped in.

"You look like a little burrito, too." I half laughed, half cried. She yawned, bringing her hand to her mouth to suckle on.

"And it must be time for dinner." I said a little louder. She turned her head to me, and stretched, as if reaching. I grabbed her little hand, such small hands, and rubbed it against my cheek.

Then, she opened her eyes slowly. I sat back in surprise. I didn't expect to be looking into such familiar green eyes.

CHAPTER 18

Gracelynn

I came to love spending time with Gracey. Even though I didn't know much about how to care for a baby, Mom had been teaching me quite a bit. My dad had said he could have Beth's aunt care for her. Both Mom and I turned him down. Legally, I was Gracelynn's guardian, and that's how it would stay.

Bobby enjoyed Gracelynn as well, and as Lane grew bigger with her child she wanted practice with Gracey. I didn't hate the idea, but I didn't like it either… so when Lane came to hold and help bottle feed or change her I was there close by, watching. Maybe I was taking it a bit far, but to me; it felt right to be close.

Going to school sucked sometimes. I still got apologies, I still had to write in my journal in the counselor's office during "free period." With so few months of school left though, I kept my grades up and did my best to stay focused.

I still worked at the diner, though not often till summer arrived again.

We were getting ready for church, and little Gracelynn wasn't cooperating. I held her close when she fussed and tried again to change and dress her. She hadn't liked her bath, and was still telling me all about it—very loudly, I may add.

My mom came in, laughing as she witnessed Gracey kicking her legs as I tried to get her pink socks on. It was a miracle I'd gotten her pink and yellow dress on the way she was fussing. The sound of my mom's voice was enough of a distraction to get the tiny socks on. I smiled, feeling successful.

"She does not like baths," I said as I carefully held her in my arms. Mom grabbed the diaper bag I'd just finished packing.

"Got everything?" she asked. I nodded. "Except the formula and bottles that are downstairs." I paused. "Oh, and Maggie." My mom smiled.

"Can't forget that!" I shook my head. Her 'Maggie' was what we called her pacifier. She had it in her mouth almost all the time, just like Maggie did in the Simpsons cartoon.

"Alright baby girl, let's go," I whispered to her as we walked downstairs.

My dad took Gracelynn happily and made silly noises at her while I put my shoes on and grabbed the rest of the stuff. After Gracelynn was safely buckled into her car seat and wrapped in her blanket, we were on our way to church. I wasn't sure how it would go; we hadn't taken her yet. I watched her fall asleep on the way, figuring all that fussing had been a work-out.

Gracelynn slept through the first half hour of church and was awake during group, so I held her while listening. Gracey seemed to like her surroundings, and the constant attention. I planned to have her baptized and my pastor was really excited about it.

Church went smoothly, and nearly everyone was in love with the baby. Bobby held her for me so I could feed her before we left, and surprised me by feeding her himself. It was cute the way he held her, smiling widely. I took her when it was time to burp and change her.

After church we went out to eat, my mom held Gracelynn while I ate and held Bobby's hand. It had been a while since I'd gone anywhere, a part of me felt good to be out...but there was another part of me that felt empty, and sad. As I ate, I wondered how long it would be before I felt normal again. I did my best to push the thoughts away and enjoy myself the best I could.

My mom and dad offered to keep Gracelynn so that Bobby and I could spend some time together. I didn't really want to, but the hopeful, excited smile on his face had me agreeing to go.

After saying "bye" to my family and kissing Gracey's cheek, Bobby held my hand and walked me toward his truck. The day was chilly, but warm in the sun. After he got in, he took my hand.

"I know it's not… easy for you yet, Katie. Thank you for trying." He smiled, the smile he saved only for me. I leaned in and gave him a quick kiss.

"What would you like to do?" I asked, looking into his fantastic eyes. He twitched his lips and then smiled as he got an idea.

"You like animals?"

I nodded, laughing. "Of course I like animals."

With a nod, we drove off. We talked little, deciding to listen to his radio.

He sang along and I couldn't help but laugh and join in. I only knew the song because of my mom. Because of her, I listen to just about everything. Bobby's smile grew wider as I joined in on his singing. His smile was very contagious.

After the song ended I looked around, not knowing at all where we were going. "Just how far away are these animals?" I asked. He gave me a lopsided grin. The one that made my mind turn to mush and my stomach feel a little funny.

"Not much farther." He turned off onto a long dirt road. There were so many trees, and I ignored the cold as I opened the window to inhale the fresh air.

"It's beautiful." I said as he came to a stop at a little ranch.

"This is my Uncle's place, AKA the farm." He helped me out of the truck. We held hands as we walked to the big red barn.

"Hey, you." A small woman with long, silver hair wrapped her arms around him. I tried to move out of the way but was grabbed next. I patted her on the back trying to introduce myself, but she cut me off.

"You are Katie! You're so beautiful!" I felt my face heat.

"Well, Aunt Fae... mind if I show her around?" Bobby asked. She pinched his cheek and I couldn't help but laugh.

"Well, you dragged her out here, better make it worthwhile!" With that, she walked away, leaving us to it.

"She seems friendly." I tucked a stray hair behind my ear. Bobby nodded in agreement and opened the barn door. I stepped in, letting him take my hand. The first thing I noticed, of course, was the smell. There were a few cows pinned up, and toward the back were horses. He stopped at the last stall and encouraged me to take a peek. As I did, I saw the cutest baby horse.

"This is Little Bit. He was born last week." Bobby said proudly.

"He's so cute!" I whispered. I got to pet him, admiring his soft pink nose.

"We have puppies in the next barn," he whispered, which made me even more excited. *Who doesn't love puppies?* After bolting the barn we walked to the smaller barn. Baby Labrador retrievers were sleeping next to their mother. They were so tiny, some black, some brown.

"Oh my gosh!" I couldn't help it. I'd always loved dogs.

"You can pet them, Big Momma doesn't bite," he assured me.

I went carefully and quietly. He was right, Big Momma couldn't have cared less that we were there. She licked both our hands and went back to sleep. I held one puppy at a time. One particular one snuggled up into my hair and Bobby took a picture of it with his phone.

"So cute," he said, looking at the photo.

After a hot cup of tea with his Aunt Fae and Uncle Lenny, we headed back to town. It was a school night after all, though neither of us had wanted to go.

"Thank you Bobby, I think I might have needed that." I said as he pulled into my driveway.

"I thought you'd have a good time." He kissed my hand, and I grabbed him in a hug.

"I love you." We said it at the same time.

After walking me to the porch and giving me a quick kiss he waited till I was inside before he left.

"Have fun?" Mom asked, cradling a sleepy Gracelynn in her arms. I nodded and smiled, but yawned. "She just ate and was changed; I was just about to put her to bed." Mom said softly. I took the baby smiling at her sleepy face.

"Thank you, Mom. I needed that." After saying goodnight I headed carefully upstairs and tucked Gracelynn into her cradle, rocking it slightly as I wound her music box. I left her door open a crack and made my way to my room.

After dressing for bed, brushing my teeth, and getting my clothes ready for school, I lay down in the cool sheets.

The day had been the best I'd had for a while and I felt thankful. I closed my eyes and thought over the day as I drifted to sleep.

CHAPTER 19

Four Months and Counting

I'd begun to count down the days left before graduation. Around one hundred and twenty-two days. I remembered when that seemed like a long time. After losing my best friend, I realized that life was short. No measure of time would make me forget… I sat down by her grave, and opened the letter I'd written. I read it out loud.

Beth,
I wake up in the morning and sometimes still have to remind myself that you're gone. Your absence leaves a giant emptiness. I don't know how I'll ever fill that hollowness, but I want you to know I'm trying. Mom packed some of your things the other day. We both cried, and had to stop. I guess we aren't ready, and that's fine. I guess it's probably normal.
Gracey is so beautiful… I paused, feeling my throat tighten, and then urged myself to go on. I held the paper a little tighter.
I show her your picture every day, and I am pretty sure she knows who you are. Beth, I don't know how to be a mom, but I want you to know I'll never give up on her as I never gave up on you…I will always do the very best that I can for her. I love you, I miss you.
K&B 4-ever.

I wiped the tears from my eyes as I folded the letter and buried it in the dirt with the other letters I'd written. I stood, blew a kiss in the air, and left.

I got to school on time even though I'd stopped to visit Beth. I grabbed my books out of my locker and smiled when Lane came up to me. She was much rounder now, and scared, but she looked happy.

"Hey," She said, smiling widely.

"Hi." I walked with her to class.

"So, it's a boy," she said with a giggle. I smiled and congratulated her.

The day went like most others. I focused on my classes. During my free period, I went to Mrs. Bradick's office.

"How are you doing?" she asked.

"I'm okay... I started writing to Beth."

Her eyes focused sadly on mine.

"Is that helping?"

"I'm not sure…I cry a lot."

"It takes time." She said, patting my knee. When I didn't say more, she handed me my notebook, and I was lost in thought for the remainder of the period.

"Hey, gorgeous," Bobby said as he sat by me at lunch.

"Hey, babe." My face lit up.

"I missed you this morning," he said, taking a drink of his water.

"I missed you, too... I stopped to visit…" he nodded before I finished, knowing where I'd been.

"Are you okay?" he asked, his hand cupping my cheek. I closed my eyes and nodded, leaning my face into his warm hand. He brushed his thumb over my lips and I sighed, opening my eyes to look into his.

"Hey, lovebirds." Lane came and sat with us, and so did her boyfriend, the baby's daddy, Drake Rickford. I didn't really like him, but I was polite, of course.

"Hey," I smiled up at them.

"How're things?" Lane arched a perfect eyebrow at me.

I shrugged and grabbed a chip. "Okay, I guess."

Lane sat next to me and Drake next to her.

"How are you guys?" I asked. Drake looked bored, but Lane smiled and grabbed his hand.

"We're good, right babe?"

"Yep."

Nice! Not a good conversationalist, I thought to myself.

"Hey, dude!" Drake said, suddenly jerking his chin up in that weird way guys say "what's up" to one of his friends that was leaving.

"Hey, man. How's it going?" I don't know the guy, he's one of the football players.

Lane rolled her eyes and smiled at me.

"I can't believe there's only four months until graduation."

I could hear the excitement in her voice. I agreed with a quick nod. "I know! Time has been going by so fast."

"I applied to Connecticut," she announced, rubbing her belly. I looked away as an image of Beth happy, healthy, and pregnant came to mind.

"That's awesome."

"Congrats!" Bobby piped up. Drake didn't seem to be paying attention, even though his friend had left.

"Well I know you'll get in, you're brilliant." I assured her.

After lunch we all went our separate ways. The rest of the afternoon went quickly, and I was walking toward the Buick with Bobby after school.

"Hey, tomorrow is my mom's birthday and we are having a little party for her... would you like to come?" I smiled.

"I'll be there." He kissed my lips softly before opening the door for me.

When I got home Gracelynn was asleep in her baby swing, Mom and Dad were napping as well, and Paul was playing a video game in his room. I went to the table and put my books down, grabbed a glass of milk and a brownie, and started on my homework. I didn't have much and it wasn't due right away, but I liked getting it done while it was fresh in my mind.

"Hi, sweetie." My mom half-whispered entering the kitchen a little later.

"Hey mom. Rough day?" I asked. She gave a half smile.

"Well, it's been a while since we've had a little one. She was cranky today because she had to have a bath."

"I hope she grows out of that soon."

"Me, too. Hey, I was thinking about just ordering some Chinese, sounds good?" Mom hardly ever ordered for delivery so I was a little surprised, but eggrolls, lo mein, and sesame chicken suddenly sounded really good. After writing down what everyone wanted a little later, she handed the list and the phone to my dad. She'd never really cared for ordering over the phone.

About thirty minutes later I put a little bit of everything on my plate and ate while feeding Gracey. My mom offered to take her, but at the shake of my head she said "You're a natural."

I took her word for it. I let Gracelynn taste a dab of the soup, and she seemed to enjoy it. After she was done eating, Mom changed her in the other room. Then, she laid Gracey on the floor with a few colorful, plush toys. After cleaning up my dishes I watched her legs kick with excitement and joined her on the floor.

Ever since Beth had passed I thought of things differently. I guess losing someone close to you really changes how you see things. I hated that she was gone, hated that she wouldn't be able to watch Gracey grow. As I looked at Grace I felt a tug on my heart. Sometimes it was hard looking at her… she looked so much like Beth already. I was actually scared of her looking exactly like Beth had when she grew up. I closed my eyes trying to clear Beth's image out of my mind again. Sometimes I hated remembering… I didn't want to hurt anymore, but I didn't know if or when it would ever stop. Sometimes the absence of her was so loud and mind boggling. And sometimes, if the doorbell rang, a tiny little part of me expected Beth to walk through the door. It wasn't fair.

I looked at Gracelynn again. I didn't even know how I could have ever been angry at her for being born. She was such a precious part of my life. Now, I couldn't imagine life without her. I hoped I'd never had to. I'd never let anything happen to her. It would be like losing Beth all over again. I shook my head at my negative thoughts, reassuring myself that Gracelynn would live a full and very happy life.

I got a phone call about an hour later. My boss asked if I could pick up a couple hours at work. I'd been more than happy to accept. When I got there I had instant tables, and was tipped really well by most. It was steady for four hours so I stayed long enough to help with clean-up. I came home with a hundred dollars in my pocket. I'd be putting it in my savings account after school, it felt nice making decent tips again.

That night once I took care of Gracelynn and got her to bed, I showered, braided my hair, set out my outfit for the next day, and said goodnight to Bobby. I slept harder than I remember sleeping for quite some time, and woke up feeling energized.

I got to school with ten minutes to spare, I ended up cuddling next to Bobby in his overly-warm truck. I didn't know if it was the heater or my hormones making it feel so hot. He had his hand in my shirt caressing the bare skin on my back. My body was on fire, but covered in goosebumps.

"You cold?" he whispered, sending a shiver down my spine.

"No, not at all. Why?"

"Goosebumps," he said, placing his lips against my ear, making me shiver again.

"Your fault." I replied. His deep laugh made my stomach flop.

"Sorry." He leaned his forehead against mine and kissed my nose. Then, he shut his truck off and we walked inside hand in hand, both wishing we were still in the quiet solitude of his truck.

Drake caught up to us and I felt a moment of panic looking at him. I didn't have to ask.

"Hospital," I guessed.

We all three went to the office and got excused from the principal. We took Bobby's truck and almost sped to the hospital. The only thing crossing my mind was a sense of déjà vu that I tried desperately to ignore.

The ride to the hospital felt like it took forever. I tried to think about anything, but I had flashback after flashback of Beth. I closed my eyes and when Beth's cold face came to mind, my eyes flew open to focus on other things. How quickly the trees moved as we drove. How Bobby's hair was extremely blonde in the bright light of day.

How Drake actually looked like he gave a crap! That was refreshing, I had to admit. He never looked like he thought of anything. I didn't like to be mean, but he always seemed like a bit of an airhead to me.

"She'll be okay," I said.

They both nodded.

"She will." Bobby smiled back at me. He probably knew that I was having a hard time with all of this.

At the hospital we waited for Bobby to find a spot to park. Drake all but ran toward the building, Bobby and I figured that we should hang back a little. Drake had the right to be there first. Besides, it gave me a little more time to collect my thoughts before I went in.

CHAPTER 20

And Here We Go Again

I called my mom to let her know that I was at the hospital with Lane, and let her know not to worry and I'd keep in touch. I sat in the waiting room with Bobby. Drake was in the room with Lane.

"You okay?" Bobby asked quietly, rubbing my hand.

"Déjà vu," I said softly. His eyes were sad so I gave a small smile. "I'm okay." Lane was in the room Beth had been in before they'd moved her. It was hard…damn near impossible to be there. I did my best to keep negative thoughts at bay.

After an hour Bobby went back to school, he had a test he couldn't miss, but he told me he'd pick up any homework for me.

"Katie?" Drake came in.

I looked up.

"Lane wants to see you."

I got up and followed him, but he shut the door and stayed in the hall so we could talk. Flashbacks hit me so hard all I wanted to do was run the hell out of there, but I took a deep breath and continued forward.

"Hey," I said, sitting beside Lane.

"Hi," she replied, rubbing her stomach.

"What happened?" I heard the crack in my voice and swallowed through it.

"Started having early contractions."

"You aren't due for a few more weeks though, right?" I asked.

"I'm already dilated to six centimeters." My mouth gaped open.

"Wow. Do you need me to do anything?" I asked, remembering that she'd wanted me for something.

"My parents are on a business trip, they are trying to find a plane home tonight, but they won't be here before this baby..." she paused as a contraction hit and I helped her focus on breathing. "Anyway, can you stay with me?"

I nodded before even really thinking about it.

"I'm scared, Katie..." I felt my throat constrict as another wave of memories flooded my mind.

"I know," I said, placing a hand on her stomach.

"You'll stay with me the whole time?" she asked.

It suddenly dawned on me that she wanted me in the delivery room with her. My eyes widened.

"Are you sure?" I asked.

"They said I can have up to two in the room if I want... I want you in there with me and Drake." She cried as another contraction hit.

A nurse came in.

"Are you ready for your epidural sweetheart?" she asked.

"Son of a bitch! Yes…" Lane yelled.

I laughed and Drake was laughing as he came back into the room.

"You staying?" he asked me while kissing Lane's hand. I nodded and moved away while a doctor came in with a huge needle.

"Holy shit!" Lane screeched scooching back a little at the sight of the epidural.

I had to bite my tongue to keep from laughing again, but even the doctor cracked a smile.

"I'll be as gentle as a feather." He winked.

"I doubt it," Lane said as she moved into a position they wanted her in.

She held Drake's hand in a vice grip. I knew from experience what that felt like, but he seemed to be doing alright. I felt bad having to sit aside while she panted through a contraction as they shoved the needle in her spine. I couldn't watch, I focused on the flecks of gray in the white tile.

"Oh my god!" Lane said as they laid her back down.

What's wrong?" Drake and I said at the same time.

"I can't feel my legs." She said it in a whiny voice.

"Completely normal, you'll thank me soon enough." The doctor reassured her. Lane already looked more relaxed.

Sitting there with Lane and Drake I did my best to stay positive. After everything that had happened with Beth… I shook my head and took a deep breath.

"Katie?" I glanced up at Lane.

"I feel like I peed," she said.

Drake pushed the nurse button and we got a quick response.

"You okay, sweetie?" the nurse asked, but then we saw a big wet spot forming around Lane. Before long everything was chaos. The nurses got their hands washed, and the doctor brought in various items and washed up.

"Time to check you, okay?" the doctor told her. Lane shrugged.

Expecting her discomfort I held her hand, but I guessed the epidural was doing its job because being checked hadn't bothered her at all. She thanked me again for staying.

"Alright, sweetheart. We are going to try a few practice pushes, things are looking good."

Lane did a few practice pushes, and leaned back, exhausted.

"Good job. We'll try again in a bit."

The contraction monitor was going crazy, but Lane barely felt anything. It made me wish Beth had gotten an epidural.

"I feel like… I need to push." Lane said, suddenly breathing heavily. Her face was covered in a sheen of sweat. Drake and I both held a hand.

"I don't…think I … can." Lane grunted.

I looked at her. I wasn't going to let anything happen to Lane.

"Lane, listen to me! Everything will be okay. I'm right here and you can do this! Be strong, alright? Stay strong." I half pleaded, half demanded, but it seemed to work because she was counting her breaths and pushing again before the doctor had to tell her to.

"Good job Lane, I see his head!" The doctor announced.

My heart skipped a beat, and Lane smiled through another push.

"Alright Lane… Take a deep breath. I want you to push as hard as you can, you're going to push and hold as I count to ten, okay?" The doctor waited for her to get ready.

Lane looked at me and I nodded, letting her squeeze my hand. "Bitch suck, shit, oh my God!" she yelled.

I figured the epidural wore off, but it was hard hiding the smile that came to my lips. She always said the funniest things.

"Shh," Drake said in an attempt to calm her down.

"Don't you dare shush me!" she yelled.

"One more time Lane, you're almost there." The doctor interrupted.

Lane pushed one more time, crying and laughing as the baby took his first breath before letting out a wail. The doctor wrapped him in the blanket and laid him in Lane's waiting arms, then he worked on doing whatever he needed down there.

It was unlike anything I'd ever seen, the moment was so beautiful, amazing really, but…it was what Beth was supposed to have experienced. What she should have had. As I looked at Lane I gave her a small smile. She held my hand.

"Thank you," she said.

I left the hospital a little while later and headed home to Gracelynn.

I held Gracey close as I told Mom all that had taken place and apologized that I hadn't texted or called her. She understood, and cried with me while I confessed it had been hard for me. I felt a little better after confiding in her. After feeding Gracelynn and laying her down with her toys I messaged Bobby.

Hey, everything went ok. Lane had her baby. I stayed in the room for the whole thing.

Hi beautiful. I'm happy for Lane, but are you ok?

Yeah, I'm alright. It wasn't easy… but I couldn't just leave her.

That's because you're an amazing person, a wonderful friend. Anyone should feel lucky to have you in their life.

Awe, thanks, I miss you.

I'll be there with your homework in about an hour… Are we still going to my mom's party together?

I'll ask! Xoxo. I didn't bother telling him that I'd kind of forgotten about the party.

"Mom, Bobby is bringing my homework by. He invited me to his mom's birthday party. Would it be okay if I go?"

She nodded. "You need to go do something fun. I'll watch Gracey."

After messaging Bobby, I hopped in the shower. I couldn't go anywhere smelling like a hospital! I put my hair in a bun after brushing it out, applied my makeup, and glanced in the mirror. I looked and felt a lot better.

Bobby was right on time as always. He brought a flower for me and stuck it in my hair. My mom took countless pictures, making me realize how many more she'd take at prom.

We got to his house, it was pretty packed. Some people I knew, and some I didn't. His mom gave me a hug and thanked me for coming. There was a ton of food and though I wasn't hungry, I ate to be polite.

After the adults began discussing things that held no interest to us, Bobby took me to his room. I looked around, paced nervously as he sat against his bed on the floor. I'd spent a lot of time with him, but it was different in his bedroom. More intimate. I slid down beside him and he nuzzled his nose in my hair. It tickled, in a pleasant way.

"You smell good," he whispered. I wondered if he knew the feelings he invoked.

"So do you," I said softly, inhaling his scent. He smelled like clean laundry and sunflower seeds. He kissed me slowly and ran his tongue against my lips, making me feel excited, nervous... alive.

CHAPTER 21

I'm Okay

Gracelynn had started learning how to squiggle on her tummy. It was adorable watching her get around. I loved listening to her making those sweet gurgling noises every time she progressed around the room. I took pictures with the camera my mom had gotten me. I took photos constantly, of Grace, my family, Bobby, friends. I wanted to capture everything I could. I smiled as Grace started making her way to me.

The first visit she had with her family doctor brought good news. The doctor had said that Gracelynn was highly intelligent for her age. She informed me that a baby's mind is a sponge and they soak everything in at this stage. My mom had already told me that. The doctor then said that Gracelynn was taking everything in at a higher pace. I was pleased to hear it and kissed Gracey's chubby pink cheek.

"Mmma" she squealed, it was time to eat. I put my camera down, scooping her up. She was getting heavier and heavier. I buckled her in her highchair and grabbed the bowl of baby rice my mom had made. It looked like something I'd find in one of her diapers.

I had to pretend to take a bite so that she would. She laughed when I made slurping noises, and finally opened her mouth. She blew little rice bubbles at me.

"I gotta go to work, Sweetie Pie." I kissed her cheek and was rewarded with a sloppy kiss as she turned her face against mine.

My mom laughed and took over feeding her so that I could get cleaned up and ready. It never took long. I said a quick "bye" to everyone and headed out the door. It was finally warming up again and I was thankful for the sun on my face. I got to work with a few minutes to spare so I made sure all the tables were clean, folded some silverware, and washed my hands.

"Morning!" My boss smiled.

"Hey, how are you?" I asked, grateful for someone to talk to.

"I'm great. You'll have a table of seven today, the reservation was called in yesterday." I busied myself getting a table set for the expected group. They arrived right at noon, and although I had my hands full with lunch rush, I enjoyed it. My older customers were always full of the latest gossip, and hearing their laughter always made my day. All of my tables tipped well, and the table of seven left me a $40.00 tip. Getting tips felt good. it wasn't about the money, it was about feeling appreciated for the job that I did.

After work I texted Mom that I was stopping at the store before coming home. I used my money to get a package of diapers, some toothpaste, and I grabbed a salad from the deli area, and ate it before driving home.

Gracelynn was napping when I got home. I quietly put the items from the store away and found Mom at the table with one of her photo albums.

"Hi, sweetheart," she said, closing the album and wiping a tear from her cheek.

"What's wrong?" I put a hand on her shoulder. She looked at me with a sad smile.

"You're growing up too fast… seems like just not long ago you were taking your first steps." She paused, opening up the album. "Look how small you were!" She pointed to a baby picture of me. I smiled and together we went through the album. When we came across an old photo of Beth and me playing in the park together I stopped to study it; taking in her bright green eyes and brilliant smile, me waving her over to play.

"It's so hard to believe I'll never see her again." I rubbed a thumb over her image, and then turned the page. I looked at my mom. "Sometimes I call her, hoping that she'll pick up the phone… I listen to her voicemail. I'm scared that one day I'll forget what she sounds like… I'm scared to forget." I paused. "Sorry…" I mumbled as I wiped my cheeks. Mom tucked a hair behind my ear, something she'd been doing for as long as I can remember.

"It's only natural, sweetheart. If you didn't mourn, I'd think something was wrong." She pecked my forehead.

"Will it ever stop hurting?"

Mom held onto my shoulder with a gentle squeeze.

"You'll always miss her honey, but what's important is to remember the good times, hang onto them."

There were a lot of both good and bad memories. I hoped I'd remember each and every one. My phone rang just then, yanking me out of memories.

"Hey Lane, what's up?"

"Hey... Um... This kid won't stop crying… I don't know what to dooo." Lane's voice broke as she joined little Malachi in tears.

"Hey... First rule, be strong." I said and she gave a pitiful half laugh. "Seriously, I don't know what's wrong!"

I nodded, I could relate to it for sure. I thought back to all those sleepless nights holding a crying Gracelynn, and trying to figure out how to stop the crying.

"Go through the list, change, feed, burp, tired, hot, or cold. Babies are weird and cry about everything."

As I listed things she began pondering, the crying in the background stopped.

"Oh my God! Thank you!" she half whispered. "He was too hot, I took off his extra blanket and socks, and he fell asleep." I smiled, feeling happy to help.

"You're welcome."

"Okay, I'm going to nap now."

I checked on Gracelynn, she was still asleep. Her plump cheeks perfectly pink, her little fingers gripping her blanket. I gently covered her peeking toes. I went to my room to clean it, which instead translated to sitting on my bed wondering why I had so much stuff.

I actually ended up cleaning; made my bed, hung my clothes up, cleaned up my desk and the top of my dresser. After feeling satisfied I lay on my bed, looking up at the white ceiling. I thought of my mom's comment, "You're growing up so fast." I realize she's right, and I realize I'll feel the same about Gracey. It's early to think about, but I do anyway.

I wonder if she'll always look like Beth, if she'll ask about her... if I'll give her a good enough life. I think I will. She won't get everything she wants, but she'll get everything she needs. She will never have to worry about the things Beth often had to worry about.

Flashbacks took me to the countless times Beth had eaten so much I thought she'd get sick, but she'd tell me she hadn't eaten for days. She used to tell me that she loved school because she was guaranteed breakfast and lunch. As she got older, she spent countless nights with us.

I remembered the times she'd cry while telling Mom and I terrible things that occurred at her house. Gracelynn wouldn't have that life, but I did hope she'd have a best friend. Someone she could talk to, listen to, get in trouble with... someone so close it would be like having a sister. I heard a small knock on the door and tried to push away my thoughts.

"Yeah?" I asked, still laying half on my bed.

"Mom says dinner is done." Paul sat beside me.

He was also growing quickly, I thought as I glanced at him. I remember when he came home from the hospital and feeling jealous because he got all the attention.

"Katie?" He said my name so quietly I almost didn't hear him.

"Hmm?"

"Are you still sad?" He looked at me, and I had the urge to cry. Instead, I swallowed hard and sat up, messing up his hair like I used to.

"I'm okay." As I said it, I knew it was true. *I was okay, even if a part of me would always hurt.*

We went downstairs together half racing to see who would get to the table the fastest, laughing when we sat at the same time. Mom and Dad even laughed.

"It's been ages since you've done that," Mom said.

I knew that she was right. We hadn't played together in a long time. I felt happy, sitting there with my family, each of us smiling widely.

I copied my brother, spinning spaghetti noodles around his fork before slurping them loudly into his mouth. I didn't slurp, but I made the "Mmm" sound as he did after swallowing. After the first couple times, I stopped copying and ate quickly. I felt more hungry than I had been for a long time.

After dinner it was the usual; clean up, and then finish any leftover homework. Since I didn't have any homework to do, I played with Gracey. I also showed her little flash cards and pointed to each one, telling her what was on each one. She loved flash card time.

Before bed, I read to her once she was in her crib. She listened intently before falling asleep.

Hey, gorgeous! I smiled at the message on my phone.

Hey yourself, how was your day?

Uneventful! Yours?

I had a pretty good day, but missed you. I smiled as I sent it.

You always miss me. He replied, making me grin even more. That was a true statement. **Look forward to seeing you tomorrow,** he added.

Me too, and yes, I do always miss you.

Goodnight, babe.

Goodnight Bobby, xo's

I laid my phone down on my nightstand, set my alarm, and got dressed for bed. Then, I laid out an outfit for the next day before brushing my teeth and went downstairs to say goodnight to my parents.

"I just don't see how she's going to raise this child and be able to focus on school. When she's in college she is going to have to work twice as hard!" I heard my dad say. I paused, where they couldn't see me. *I felt a little guilty standing there listening in on them, but they were obviously talking about me!*

"Dear, she'll be fine! We'll keep Gracey with us, she can see her anytime."

"I think the child belongs with her actual family."

I felt a lump form in my throat. *The child? Actual family?* My face heated in anger. How could my dad not see that I am her family? Gracey is mine! I went back to my room and closed the door. I wanted to slam it as hard as I could. I wanted to go back down and yell at him. I was hurt, and angry. I wouldn't give Gracelynn up, Ever!

CHAPTER 22

The Fuse Has Been Lit

The next morning I did my routine early. I hadn't slept well, going to bed angry had that effect on me. I changed, and fed Gracey before putting her in a new outfit. Mom took over so I could eat breakfast. I wasn't hungry, and when I saw my dad sitting there with his coffee and paper I felt angrier than before.

"Morning, Pickle," he said, barely looking at me. I stood there like an idiot, unable to respond or move. "Do you need something?" Dad asked, glancing away from his paper to study me. I shook my head, but my fists were clenched. I had to go.

"Bye," I said to no one in particular before I stormed out to get in the Buick. I warmed the car up, blasted the stereo, and drove to school thirty minutes early.

I parked in my usual spot, closest to the old oak tree. My head was full, my heart pounding in my ears. I can't remember a time I was so angry at my dad. I turned the car off, got out and locked up, slinging my backpack over my right shoulder.

The air smelled sweet, and the rush of wind on my face made me feel a little better. Nature usually had that influence on me. I was still angry for sure, but I no longer felt like chewing someone out and acting like an idiot.

I remember Beth once saying I was like a firecracker. Once the fuse was lit, you didn't know how or when I'd pop. I had laughed at her because I hardly ever got mad.

The parking lot became crowded after a while and when Bobby pulled in. I felt that warm, familiar flutter in my stomach.

"You must have come pretty early," he said, wrapping an arm around my waist and pulling me close. The smell of sunflower seeds filled my nostrils and I sighed.

"Bad morning." I told him what I'd heard and looked up at him as I waited for his reply.

"Wow..." he finally responded.

"Yeah. I mean... How could he say something like that?" I felt hurt all over again, but it was nice to get it off of my chest.

"Well, Katie... Maybe he's just worried." Bobby said as we walked inside.

"Worried or not, Gracey is my responsibility. I'm... *we're* her family. Even though I'm only seventeen, I know I can do it." I waited while he grabbed a book from his locker.

"Yeah, but from his point of view I think he just wants you to succeed, and the baby is, well it's a lot to handle when you need to be focusing on your future."

I raised my eyebrows at him. *Was he really siding with my dad?*

"So, you think he's right?" I put a hand on my hip. (Something I always tended to do when I was getting upset.)

"Well... he has a right to how he feels is all." Bobby turned to face me and I suddenly felt worse than I had when I got here.

"Whatever. I gotta go." I turned around, forcing myself to walk away.

"Katie!" he called out. I kept walking, not looking back.

Most of the day I kept to myself, I even ate lunch in the counselor's office. Bobby hadn't attempted to talk to me, and I was glad. I didn't like being mad at him, suddenly realizing that this was the first time I had ever really been mad at him.

After school I left quickly, not waiting for Bobby as I always did. I felt a ping of gloom and guilt. I could imagine him walking out and feeling sad that I'd left. When I got home, I took my time getting inside. I knew I'd need to talk about what I'd heard. Once I put my things in my room I went downstairs to find Gracey doing tummy time on the floor. I kissed her cheek and got a glass of water from the kitchen, where Mom was checking on her lasagna. It smelled good, as always.

"Hey sweetie, how was your day?" She always asked me how my day was, but today, it forms a lump in my throat and I know I'm about to cry.

"Well…" I chewed on my lip to keep it from trembling. Mom rushed to my side, asking if I was okay.

"I heard…"

"Heard what, sweetheart?"

Mom's face was full of concern, which somehow made it harder to talk. "Heard what Dad said. Last night, about Gracey."

Mom's eyes grew wide and she let out a breath. "Oh, honey! I'm sorry you heard all that! He didn't mean it to be mean... He's worried about you, that's all." Mom rubbed my back as I fought back tears. I stood and shook my head.

"I'm fine." I went upstairs leaving my mom to worry by herself.

After spending an hour with Gracelynn I felt a little better. When she fell asleep, I went to my room and closed the door. I checked my phone. Two missed calls, one new voicemail, and three text messages. I flopped on my bed and listened to the voicemail.

"Hey Katie.. It's me. I just wanted to say I'm sorry. I didn't mean to make you mad. Please call me… if you want. Bye." He sounded so sad it made me feel even worse for being mad at him. When I heard my dad come home though, I shot out of bed heading downstairs, temporarily forgetting being upset at Bobby.

"Hey, Pickle!" he said, hanging up his coat.

I frowned, crossing my arms.

"You're upset, I assume." He asked.

I raised my eyebrows.

"Katie, it's been a long day and I'm exhausted. I don't have the energy for silly games." He started walking away.

"I'm her family! We are her family!" I finally said. Still standing on the bottom step. That got his attention.

"Who?"

"Gracelynn! Dad, I'm her family. I will not let you take her from me." He started to talk but I shook my head. "I get good grades, I take care of myself, I help pay for things I need and want. I don't drink, smoke, have never done drugs. I always do everything I can to make you and Mom happy. I think I deserve a little more credit from you!" I had begun to cry.

"You're a child trying to take care of a child!" Dad shouted. He didn't like when I was emotional.

"I'm not a child anymore! I can take care of that little girl!" I turned and ran to my room slamming the door. I'd never yelled at my dad like that, never made him feel bad intentionally… he'd never disappointed me so much.

Not long after the argument, there was a tap on my door.

"Yeah?" I croaked my throat raw from yelling and crying.

My mom sat on the edge of my bed. I didn't want to talk, I didn't want to see the look of disappointment or hurt that was most likely showing on her normally happy face.

"Are you alright?" Mom asked.

I risked a glance at her. It wasn't what I'd expected her to say. I felt sad, and guilty on top of feeling hurt and angry.

"I'm sorry." I wiped at a tear that tickled the end of my nose. Mom nodded. "He just…"

"Made you mad? Hurt your feelings? Disappointed you?" She seemed to read my mind. I nodded.

"All three," I said, and a small smile tugged at the corner of her mouth.

"Your fit was uncalled for." She gave me a stern look before she continued. "However, you stood up for yourself and for that baby girl. You stood up for what you wanted. I know that wasn't easy."

I wasn't sure how to feel. I hadn't expected her to be nice, and I definitely didn't think she'd be proud either.

"I feel bad for yelling at him like that, but he really hurt me saying what he said. I just... Blew up."

She nodded again, patting my leg. Then, she left, shutting the door quietly behind her. I grabbed my phone and sighed as I waited for Bobby to pick up.

"Hey." His voice was pleasant and welcoming.

"Hi," I replied softly. "I'm so sorry, I wasn't mad at you. I feel terrible about today, I was being so childish!" I said it quickly, almost in one breath.

"It's alright. I know you were mad. I'm sorry too. Sometimes I don't always say the right thing, or maybe I just don't think about it before I say it. Are you and your dad okay?"

I thought for a minute.

"I'm not sure. I kinda blew up at him. He yelled, I yelled. It really wasn't pretty." He was quiet while I talked.

"Everything will be okay. Look, I hate to do this, but I have to go. Gotta eat dinner and do homework. I'll see you in the morning?"

"Okay... Thank you Bobby, for everything."

"You're welcome, beautiful. Goodnight."

"Goodnight." I hung up and sank back against the pillows feeling at least a little better. Another knock on my door had me sitting up and alert.

"Come in," I said softly, knowing it was my dad. He came in and sat on the chair across from me. He looked depressed, I hated it. I tucked a hair behind my ear nervously.

"Dad, I'm sorry for yelling at you. I should have calmed down before telling you how I felt, instead of throwing a childish tantrum like that." He looked at me and gave a small nod.

"I know that you are no longer a child." He scratched his chin like always when thinking. "You're not a child, but you'll always be my baby. My little girl. This whole thing has been hard on you, hard on all of us. A baby is a big thing."

"I know," I agreed.

"I know you can do this, Pickle… As your parent, I can't help but worry. I hope you know that I do trust you, and am very proud of you. You have grown up so much, and you are doing an amazing job."

He gave me a hug, and left. I stared at the closed door, the silence pounding in my ears. I felt better, although emotionally exhausted.

CHAPTER 23

Panic Begins To Set In

Time had this unexpected way of flying by without my realizing how quickly it was happening. What used to be months away was now right around the corner. Finals were coming, prom was coming... Graduation was coming.

I sat in the parking lot and stared at the red brick building. I remember a time when I was so ready to just be done with it. The school, most of the people… now that the time was approaching, I was kind of freaking out a bit. Bobby's truck came into view and I let out a pent-up breath.

Walking hand in hand across the parking lot, I let the morning sun warm me and cleared my thoughts. Being worried, freaking out, or being frustrated wouldn't do anything good for my day. I had to stay calm, collected, and focused. Bobby gave my hand a kiss as we walked inside.

"Wait for me!" I turned to see Lane sprinting toward us. I couldn't help but laugh. Her hair was a mess, her makeup far from the normal perfection, and her outfit didn't even match.

"Hey," I said, trying to sound cheery.

"Stop gawking! I know I look like total shiot! Mal didn't sleep well, and that means I didn't either!" she pouted. I nodded in sympathetic understanding. I'd had my share of late nights with Gracelynn. We entered the building together and then, we went our separate ways.

"Three months isn't a long time." I told the school counselor as I sat in my usual spot. I hadn't meant to say it out loud. She looked at me, waiting for me to continue.

"I mean…The months used to seem so long. School is almost over, I'll be off to college, and raising a child… it's not far from now."

She crossed her legs and swiveled her chair to fully face me. It was kind of annoying when she did that, but I never said as much.

"No… When we grow up, time has a way of moving differently. You have a lot on your plate." I nodded, taking a deep breath.

"I'm scared." I admitted.

She nodded again and patted my hand. "It's normal to be scared. There is a whole new unexplored world out there waiting for you. The baby is a big change, college is a big step. Katie, are your parents keeping her while you're in school?"

I nodded, and she studied me for a moment before continuing.

"They have programs to help you, you know? Some colleges have babysitting so you'd be able to take her with you. If that's something you'd like to try… I will be honest with you and say that I think your parents taking her would be better for you both."

I looked up at her. *Did she think I couldn't handle it?*

"I think you'd be able to get more from college without having an extra worry. Your education has to be taken into account," she said, almost as if she were reading my mind. I tried to see it from her and my parents' perspectives.

"Beth gave me this baby. She gave me this big responsibility, this beautiful piece of her." I watched Mrs. Bradick move to sit by me and she gave me a hug.

"I know it's hard."

I shook my head, wiping at the tears. "You don't! No one knows how much this hurts, how hard it is. Gracey is my responsibility. How can I just leave her behind and act like it's no big thing? How can I take her with me and be in college?" I stood.

"This isn't something I can just decide." I grabbed my bag and walked out before the bell rang. The rest of the day I tried to focus on my assignments, my head swimming with thought.

"You don't have to choose today," Lane said as we walked toward our vehicles. I nodded. I knew she was right, I still had some time to decide what I wanted, what would work best for me, for Gracey. Bobby caught up and laced his fingers through mine. They felt warm, comforting. Lane left and I leaned against my car still holding Bobby's hand.

"I'm sorry for getting upset with you," I apologized again for the umpteenth time. He rolled his eyes and tilted my chin to look in my eyes.

"It will be okay, and I forgave you for it. You have a lot on your mind. I understand, and I'm here for you." I leaned into him, putting my head against his chest.

"I love you," I whispered. I heard his heart race and I glanced up to see him smiling.

"I love you, too." We kissed, and it felt light as a feather before growing into a heated flame. I pulled away after a while, both of us taking in gulps of air.

"I want to kiss you every minute of every day." He whispered, placing his arms around my waist. My body became electric against him.

"I better go." I said, willing my mind and body to agree with my words. He nodded, and kissed me lightly before opening my door for me. "I'll call you later, babe."

I smiled as he shut the door, and took a deep breath. Suddenly I was thinking about a lot more than the baby, and college. I wish I could talk to Beth about these thoughts. When it came to my hormones I didn't really want to talk about it with my parents. I could hear it now. *No thanks!* I took another calming breath before I headed home.

I didn't have much time before I had to go to work. I chose to lie on the floor with Gracey. She was playing, and still had one of her rattles in her hand when she turned to study me. She was such a good baby. I ran my finger against her cheek.

"Hi, beautiful," I said softly.

She yawned and smacked her lips, as she turned her face toward me. She looked tired. I couldn't help but laugh, and wonder how she could sleep so much.

Both my mom and the doctor told me to expect her napping to decrease as she learned to crawl. Judging by her success during tummy time, I didn't think it would be much longer before she'd be taking over the house.

I got up and changed for work a little after that, and gave my mom a hug before grabbing the keys to the Buick. I threw my jacket on and headed out.

"Hey, how are you? How's that beautiful baby?"

I smiled at my boss. "I'm good, and she's gorgeous. She looks a lot like her mom."

My boss gave a sympathetic smile before changing the subject. I liked that about her, she never pried.

"We are probably in for a slow night, but feel free to find cleaning to do. Hate to send you home too early."

I nodded, she knew I was saving up for college and a Jeep, so she always tried to keep me as long as she could. I wasn't too worried about that, though. I had so much to think about as it was.

"It's okay, send me home when you need to. Between Gracey, school, and thinking about college I have plenty to keep myself occupied."

"And your boyfriend!" She smiled, wiggling her eyebrows.

I felt my face heat.

"Yeah, and Bobby." I tried to stop blushing.

"How are you two getting along?" she asked, piling a stack of plates on the counter.

"Good, we're both pretty busy but we still try to go out when we can."

"That's good," she replied as she cleaned a table.

"I wish we had more time together though."

"Yeah, senior year can take its toll, I remember those days." I rolled my eyes, making her laugh.

"Well, I'm here for you if you ever need to talk." She patted my arm.

"Thanks." I thought about that for a little while as I took my time cleaning and rearranging. *Maybe I could talk to her about my feelings, about Bobby.* I blushed at the thought, but still. *She was young, easy to talk to.* I had always felt comfortable around her, and I had known her for quite a long time. I felt like I could trust her about that subject.

"Katie?" My eyes snapped up to look at her.

"You okay?"

I nodded. "Yeah, I was just thinking."

"Would you like to talk?"

I appreciated her wanting to talk to me, but at the same time I was nervous about the topic at hand.

"Well, it's about Bobby," I said slowly.

She nodded, and we sat in a booth with a snack and our drinks. I played with my straw as I contemplated how to go about the conversation.

"Are you guys fighting?" she asked, placing a hand on my arm.

"No... Nothing like that." I paused and took a breath.

"How did you know you were… you know… ready?"

She looked at me vacantly for a moment until it registered what I was asking. "Oh... Um. You should..." I shook my head to stop her.

"I really need a friend."

She nodded again, seeming to understand.

"Well, I wasn't really sure when it happened, but it was with my husband, before we got married. I guess he made me feel safe and happy. I was comfortable with him, and knew he was who I wanted to marry." I pondered her answer. It was pretty typical to keep mentioning marriage.

"I've just been having these crazy wild feelings when we're together. He feels it too, but I know we wouldn't do anything unless we were both ready." She raised her eyes and smiled kindly. "Bobby is a good guy. I know he'd never pressure me or anything." She patted my arm again.

"It's best to wait until you are absolutely positive that it's what you want. It isn't something you can ever take back."

I nodded. "A part of me wants to now, but... I look at Gracey and think about Beth…"

"Sweetheart, Beth may not have done what was best for her. She didn't have the same upbringing, the parents that you have." I felt a lump rise in my throat, and willed myself not to cry.

"I wish I could talk to her..." My lip quivered and I took a calming breath.

"I know, and I wish that too." I cleared my throat and stood.

"Katie?"

"Yeah?"

"Just...be sure you're ready."

I smiled and nodded as she got up. I got back to my cleaning, as she cleaned up our snack.

We didn't have a big dinner rush, and after cleaning up I got to go home. I took my time, driving slowly. The evening was cold, but welcoming.

I decided to tool around town before going home. It didn't take long before I was home, though. I parked in the driveway and shut off the engine. As I sat there, looking at the house, I realized I really didn't feel like being home.

I went inside and changed out of my uniform, and bundled up Grace. She kicked her feet excitedly when I strapped her in the stroller. Mom laughed and handed me her blanket and I snuggled her in it. Then, we headed out. The first star came into view. I watched it twinkle as I walked. More stars came into view, the first larger, and seemingly brighter. I couldn't help but wonder if Beth was somewhere up there, in the vast deep space, watching me.

Probably not, but it was comforting to think so. They say when you die your spirit floats up and away, like you're sleeping but you just never wake up. At least that's how I interpreted that conversation in Bible study.

I pushed the stroller slowly, looking at the sky and then back down at Gracelynn who was taking in the sights around her. I don't normally take her out in the evening, it's a bit chilly, so I turn around after a couple of blocks.

When we got back to the house I locked the stroller before picking up Gracey and snuggling her close to me.

"I miss you, Beth." I said to the sky, wondering if maybe she knew that already. I had an urge to cry, and before I could stop it the tears were streaming down my face. I held Gracey just a little closer, and took her inside.

CHAPTER 24

Prom

Time continued to soar by. I was silently panicking, and wondered if anyone else knew how I felt. My mom and I were at the mall shopping for my dress. I remembered Beth and I looking at dresses just for fun, she'd said "I'll wear something... like a suit, and you can be girly if you want. We can go together, dance like idiots, I'll spike the punch, and we'll leave." Her words echoed in my mind, it seemed so real that I almost expected her to be standing right beside me.

Mom held up a deep green dress, about knee length, the kind that flared out when you spun. I shook my head. It was pretty, but I wanted to wear blue because it was Bobby's favorite color.

"Still set on blue?" I nodded and my mom sighed, putting away a pretty red floor-length gown.

"Blue is a popular color." I knew she wasn't happy.

"I know... But Bobby is wearing a black tux with a blue tie."

She smiled. "I can't believe you're going to prom! Already!"

I shrugged, then, just when I was turning to another rack of dresses. I saw it. It was beautiful. Deep blue, floor length, spaghetti strap, had an open back, it was sparkly, and perfect. I grabbed it, it was my size! I actually squealed. My mom's eyes lit up as I put it against me.

"Oh! That's gorgeous! Go try it on."

We found an empty dressing room and I slowly pulled the dress on. The fabric was soft, and hugged my body in a nice way. I stared at myself in the mirror. I felt beautiful. I took a breath, tucked a hair behind my ear, and walked out.

"Oh, honey! It's perfect!" I spun and giggled with my mom, allowing myself to have this moment. "Certainly worth one hundred and sixty!" she continued. I smiled even more widely.

After picking out the dress shoes, we looked at hair accessories, makeup, and jewelry. I grabbed some new eye shadow; some blues and grays that would go with the dress. I found a hair clip that danced in the light, and Mom picked out a pretty necklace, it was a simple chain with a pretty blue stone in the center. I hadn't expected my mom to spend so much on me for prom, but as I looked at her I saw how happy she seemed.

"Thank you, Mom."

"You're welcome, sweetheart."

When we got home she helped me carry the things to my room. She hung the dress in my closet while I unpacked the make-up we'd picked out. With the eye shadow I'd also gotten eyeliner, silvery glitter, and a pretty lip gloss that is supposed to make your lips a light strawberry color and taste like strawberries. It's called strawberry passion. I hope it actually works because it was pretty expensive. As I put it and everything else in my make-up box I felt like trying the lip gloss on. I didn't allow myself, I wanted everything to be kept in great condition before the big night.

I took Gracelynn from dad, and smiled as she cuddled into me. "Was she good today?" I asked him.

"She was great," Dad said with a smile, though he seemed worn out.

I took Grace to the living room with her toys for tummy time. She squealed with delight when she pressed on her teddy bear and it sang to her. I played with her feet, her giggling making me laugh. Spending time with Gracelynn made each day special.

Mom and I made tacos for lunch a while after. I enjoyed taco making. I set out bowls full of different items like black olives, diced tomatoes, cheese, refried beans, sweet green onions, and lettuce. Then, I set out the sour cream, salsa, and a bottle of ranch. I put it all on the table. After the hamburger was ready we put it out, and put the tortillas on the open flame so they'd have that perfect warmth.

Paul and Dad rushed to the table before I had finished setting the table. I grabbed the glasses and a bottle of sparkling apple juice. Lunch was amazing.

I sat beside Gracey, laughing as she squished some beans and rubbed them on her mouth and cheeks as she said "Mmm" in approval. She'd need a bath after this.

Gracelynn had finally warmed up to her bath time. Now-a-days it was hard to get her out of it. I snuggled her in a soft, fluffy pink towel and took her to her room. As I got her ready for her nap she smiled up at me with sparkling eyes. If I looked closely I could see small flecks of golden-brown through the green.

"You're so beautiful," I told her as I watched her kick her legs in excitement at my voice, and I couldn't help but to feel happy at that moment.

When I finished, I made a bottle and fed her before laying her down. Then, I took a long shower, allowing the hot water to beat against me before I shut it off. The rest of the day went quickly and that night after saying goodnight to Bobby and getting clothes ready for school, I looked out the window.

The sky was lit by a stunning full moon, and the stars seemed to dance in front of my eyes. Sleepier than I'd been before, I laid down and relaxed into my bed.

I smacked my alarm harder than necessary. I'd had one of those nights where you felt like you just got to sleep and the alarm went off. I threw the covers over my head, mumbling and fighting myself to wake up. I just didn't feel like it. My buzzer went off again, and I must have pressed the snooze. I flung the covers off and pushed the off button.

"Fine! I'm up!" I said grumpily to the empty room. I didn't take long dressing and brushing out my hair. I put a head-band on deciding that I didn't want to fuss with it. Then, I walked downstairs.

My mom surprised me with a waiting cup of coffee. I rubbed my eyes, looking again to see if maybe I'd been imagining it. *Nope! It was real!* I grabbed it and took a sip.

"Ooh. Thank you." I said after swallowing.

My mom laughed, and put some scrambled eggs on a plate before handing them to me.

"Thanks, Mom."

"You're welcome. You don't look like you slept well." She said, studying me with her worried "mom face."

I shrugged, taking in another gulp of coffee and following it with a fork full of eggs.

"Are you alright, sweetheart?" Mom looked at me with serious eyes and rubbed my arm.

"I just… everything is moving so fast. I can't believe it's almost prom. Can't believe I have a date… can't believe Beth won't be there with me." I took a deep breath. "We talked about it a few times… two loser friends going together." I laughed at the thought.

Mom smiled sadly. "It's been a rough year. I'm proud of the woman you're becoming."

I felt myself begin to tear up so I forced a smile. "Thanks." I got up and rinsed my plate before putting it in the dishwasher.

"I'd better get to school." I walked to the living room where Gracelynn was sleeping and kissed her plump cheek, earning a soft sigh. I headed out.

I leaned against the Buick in my usual spot as I waited for Bobby and Lane. I closed my eyes, soaking in the sun. It was a nice morning. I'd always loved spring. Loved the flowers that graced everyone's yards, the brilliant greens of the grass and the trees. Loved how blue the sky was, and how sweet the air smelled.

Bobby laced his fingers through mine as he walked me to class. Thoughts churned through my mind as we silently walked hand in hand. How so many things had changed and how others hadn't. The building smelled the same, the teachers looked the same; preserved timelessly from kindergarten. Lane came into step beside me and smiled.

"I can't believe it's almost over! Prom is tomorrow!" she squeaked excitedly, making Bobby jump.

We parted ways. I wasn't looking forward to finals, but I knew I'd manage.

The day went by in a frantic blur. Everyone was buzzing with end-of-the-year energy. Seniors clapped when the final bell rang. Of course, there were a couple days off before we'd get our final grades. Then, we'd walk the stage, grab our certificates… and it would be over.

As much as I was kind of glad to be finished, I felt worried. Having Gracey thrown into my life in the way she was, I guess it made sense. I mean… I wasn't even eighteen and I already had a daughter. As I looked at Lane standing beside me, eager to get home to Malachi (her beautiful boy) I felt kind of relieved. I wasn't the only one who was going through this.

I said "Bye" to Lane and walked toward Bobby, who smiled dreamily in my direction. I couldn't help but look away as my face heated.

He nuzzled my neck, making me giggle.

We planned on going to the movies. I didn't know what we were going to watch, and honestly we were probably just going to make out, so I didn't really care. I thoroughly enjoyed making out with Bobby. We kissed, and I went home to spend time with Gracey before getting ready for my date.

I dressed in jeans and a cute white top with what they call elephant sleeves. Its thin material tickled nicely against my skin. I left my hair down, and dabbed a little perfume on my wrists and neck. After saying my goodbyes to my family, I waited on the porch.

Bobby was right on time as always, and we went to the movies hand in hand. I took off my jacket and blushed as Bobby gave me the once over.

"God, you're beautiful!" he whispered. My skin tingled as I flushed, my arms suddenly covered in tiny goosebumps.

"Thank you." I whispered, trying to calm my racing heart. We found our seats, choosing the balcony in the very back. It wasn't really crowded so it was nice. We were basically all alone, which made our make out session more enjoyable. Bobby stroked my cheek with soft fingers taking me from my thoughts.

"I'm so in love with you." He brushed his lips against mine before I could reply.

My body responded to his touch, he was like a magnetic force. I ran a hand through his hair, feeling my body tremble as his kiss deepened. We both wanted so much more, but we also both wanted to wait. It was kind of perfect. I couldn't help but feel lucky.

After our date Bobby took me home. We sat in his truck for a while, kissing a little longer. I couldn't ever get enough of it, enough of him.

"See you tomorrow night. I'll pick you up at seven." He nuzzled my neck again, making me feel all fuzzy inside. I nodded and kissed him once again before heading in.

"Have a good time?" I grabbed my chest and giggled. I hadn't seen my mom sitting on the couch.

"Sorry, didn't mean to scare you."

I shook my head.

"It's okay. I had a good time. Thank you."

"You and Bobby are getting pretty serious." She studied my face, and I only nodded while I took off my jacket.

"Sweetheart, I want to talk about prom night."

I felt my heart race and my stomach do a little flip, not really looking forward to the conversation. I sat beside her and waited for her to give the inevitable speech.

"Prom night is fun, almost magical with its music, and dancing, but you're going to feel other things too, and there are other kids that might talk about getting rooms…" She cleared her throat.

I nodded. "I know."

"You and Bobby… are you being safe?" she asked, raising a brow. I felt my face get at least ten shades of red.

"Mom… we haven't... I mean… we aren't..." I shrugged, hoping I wouldn't have to just outright tell her I was still a virgin.

"Oh!" Her smile grew. "Honey, I just wanted to make sure. I mean, I know how prom night is."

"Well, it's really cliché and stupid... I mean, we… we aren't ready for that."

My mom nodded in obvious delight. She gave me a hug, and busied herself with dinner while I went upstairs to change.

That night, I thought about prom, about Bobby. I thought about graduation and college. I thought about life even further out than that. *How would it be? Would Bobby and I still be together?* I hoped so. I closed my eyes and let my thoughts fade to dreams.

Time seemed to move so slowly up until go time. I had spent the day playing with Gracelynn, I took her for a walk, we played with flash cards, and I read her a book. When Dad took over with Gracey, I looked at the clock. It was time to get ready for prom.

"You look so beautiful!" my mom cried, and wiped at a stray tear. I hugged her, feeling nervous, excited, and scared all at once.

"Thanks, Mom."

She got up and sprayed what felt like half a can of hairspray to hold my curls in place. So much that my hair actually went CRUNCH when you touched it. *Nice!* I could see it now, Bobby would touch my hair or something and it would be crunchy. I didn't complain though, because looking at my reflection, I felt brand-new. I felt stunning, and I liked the feeling.

My dress fell delicately around me, hugging onto curves I'd never noticed before. I'd spent a long time on my makeup, longer than I'd ever planned on. I heard the doorbell and my heart suddenly hammered in my chest.

"He's here!"

Mom walked with me down the stairs. Bobby looked handsome in his suit and tie, and my heart skipped.

"You're gorgeous!" he said, taking my arm. He gave me a corsage, and gave my mom a rose.

My mom snapped a billion pictures, my dad tried to be cool but I could see him tear up. Paul high-fived Bobby and I before going back to his games. I kissed Gracey, and then, we were off. After my mom had whispered to me not to do anything I didn't want to, and my dad gave Bobby the staredown of his life, we both laughed about it on the way to school.

"You really look amazing," Bobby said in the all-too-quiet truck.

"Thank you. You do, too," earning me a brilliant smile.

It was beautiful. Blues and silvers. So many balloons and streamers. Candles and flowers gracing tables as centerpieces. They really did a good job. A big fancy transformation from the usual smelly gymnasium, and it was loud, but the music wasn't cheesy. We got our picture taken almost instantly, then he swept me toward the dance floor. I didn't know he could dance, but it was a happy surprise. I wondered, *had his mom taught him?*

My mom and dad had both taught me. It was much different, though. Stupidly, I felt like Cinderella dancing with her prince. Bobby held me close, closer than ever, and my stomach was flopping as quickly as my heart was beating. I wondered if he felt the same. After a while, it sort of felt like we were alone. The crowd seemed to have faded away as he kissed me softly.

"Hey! You look amazing!" Lane's voice cut through the magic and I turned to face her. She wore a beautiful, black satin dress that seemed to move as if it were extra skin.

"So do you." She was swept away before we could say anything else.

"Want some water?" Bobby asked. I nodded and I sat at an empty table while he grabbed us a drink. It felt so surreal, and in that moment, I wanted nothing more than to see Beth taking over the dance floor.

After prom we went to our place and looked at the stars. He'd laid a blanket in the bed of his truck. We laid side by side. Holding hands. He'd kissed me, but neither one of us tried for anything more. Even though we wanted to.

"Thank you for tonight. It was perfect."I told him as he snuggled close.

"You're perfect," he whispered. Then, with a soft kiss he added "I love you."

My smile grew as I looked into his eyes. "I love you, too."

He took me home and walked me to the door, kissing me again before he left. "See you tomorrow, beautiful."

I felt my face heat. "Goodnight Bobby, it was wonderful."

Once inside I shut the door and my mom hugged me, and then helped take the pins out of my hair. It fell heavily against my back, and I wanted nothing more than to get in the shower. I studied myself one last time before I took the dress off and let the hot water work its charm.

CHAPTER 25

Graduation

The practice graduation seemingly took all day, and the senior jocks were acting stupid. When it was my turn I walked across the stage, grabbed my fake diploma, which was a rolled-up piece of computer paper, and shook my principal's hand.

"Well done, Katie!" he said loudly, making my face heat in embarrassment.

I mumbled "Thank you," and took a seat beside Lane, who'd already taken her turn. I smiled as I watched Bobby grab his fake diploma and take a bow before sitting beside me.

"I can't believe we're graduating in two days!" Lane squeaked.

I nodded, only slightly enthused. "This year went quickly," I agreed.

Bobby took my hand before adding, "It had a lot of ups and downs...but I'm happy and I have few regrets."

"I miss her so much," I said after a while.

Lane patted my shoulder. "I miss her too. She was an awesome person, and a good friend. I wish I would have gotten to know her better."

Bobby cupped my cheek in his soft, warm hand and wiped a tear away. "She's with you in here." He put his hand against my heart.

"I know... And I see her every day when I look at Gracelynn. I just...wish she was here. Wish she could have experienced much more. She had a whole life ahead of her." I took a steady breath.

"She had so much more to do in life… so much more to accomplish." Bobby hugged me again, and Lane wiped at a few of her own tears.

"I should have hung out with you guys… instead of waiting for it to become convenient. You were both such a big help to me," Lane added.

"I was jealous when she started spending time with you," I admitted.

Lane glanced at me. "I didn't want to leave you out, but I didn't know how to include you either, not at first."

"I'm glad I got to know you." I assured her.

"Me too."

Bobby stood and helped me up. Practice was finally over. We single-filed our way out of the gym and we all excitedly left. I said bye to Lane, and Bobby followed me home. He came inside with me, my mom gave him a hug and Paul ambushed him about a new video game.

"Maybe in a bit, buddy," he replied. That made Paul happy. He loved Bobby. I grabbed Gracey from Mom and played with her in the living room.

"She really does look a lot like her," Bobby said as he laid beside me on the floor. Gracelynn smiled sweetly at him.

"I know." I tried to sound natural, but I knew my voice held the pain I felt.

Bobby squeezed my hand. "Have you decided what to do?" he asked me softly, not looking at me.

I shrugged. "I put in my college apps, just waiting now. Looking forward to the summer with Gracelynn, and you." I nudged him with an elbow.

"We'll have an awesome summer, and we'll figure out the rest later," Bobby said as he placed his hand on mine. I raised my eyebrows in agreement before turning my attention back to Gracey.

Bobby went home after playing some games with Paul and I replayed the conversation in my head. Mom came in, handing me an envelope, I broke out of my thoughts long enough to read it.

Dear Katie,

It's been a while since I've written and I wanted to apologize. I was sick with the flu for a couple weeks. Thank you for the picture of sweet, little Gracelynn. My, she sure looks so much like Beth did.

I understand you don't want to give Grace to me, and it's okay, but I'd like to see her in person if that's alright? Have you decided what to do about college? I'm sure you'll figure something out. Beth told me you're the smartest and wisest person she'd ever met. You were very special to her. I'm sure you know that.

Well, let me know what you think about me coming for a visit. I was thinking about next month. Hope to hear from you soon.

Beck.

I folded the letter and put it back in the envelope carefully. I glanced at Mom, who had taken over playing with Gracelynn while I'd read the letter.

"She wants to see her."

"Was...well...is she coming here?" My mom stuttered.

I shrugged. "I have to write her back. I'm not sure what to think, though. I've only met her a few times. She's nice, but..."

Mom nodded as she bounced Grace on her leg. "Well, she is Gracelynn's aunt. From what I've heard she is a good person. Beth trusted her."

I studied Gracelynn's smiling face. She needed family. "I'm sure it would be okay," I decided.

"Good. It's time for this little girl to have a bath." With that, she carried her off.

Mom always knew when I needed to be alone. I read the letter again, and then stared at the ceiling fan. The blades moved slowly, and as I watched them I began to feel the day catch up to me.

Sometime later my eyes drifted open and I sat up, my back stiff from falling asleep on the floor. The smell of bacon lingered in the air, enticing my empty stomach. Standing and stretching, I made my way to the kitchen. Mom was making BLTs. I couldn't remember if I'd eaten at all, but judging by the noise my stomach was making, I must not have.

"Morning," Mom teased.

"I didn't mean to fall asleep."

She handed me a plate. I assembled my BLT with extra T, light on the B, and a glob of mayo. After sprinkling the tomato with some salt and pepper, I put potato chips on my plate, grabbed a Sprite from the fridge, and joined Paul at the table.

Dad joined us and Mom set his plate on the table in front of him.

"Mmm, bacon!" We all laughed. Dad had a thing for bacon. Once Mom sat down with her plate, Dad and I began to eat. We always waited for Mom. My sandwich tasted amazing, I ate quickly, loving every bite.

"Goodness, someone's hungry!" I looked up to find everyone watching me eat.

"I'm not sure if I ate anything today," I finally said after swallowing.

After I ate another BLT, I helped Mom clean up, and then went up to my room. Gracelynn was occupied with Mom and Dad, and Paul had returned to his usual video games.

Up in my bedroom I laid on my bed, enjoying the quiet solitude. I glanced at my new dress. Deep blue, shimmering in the last bit of sunlight peeking through my curtains. I'd gotten it with Mom. She'd complimented my taste, and had cried when I put it on. As I looked at it, I felt like crying. I'd be wearing it under my gown at the graduation ceremony. My stomach did a flop and I suddenly regretted that second BLT.

I stood and went to the bathroom for a couple Antacids. After popping two in my mouth, I went back to bed. I knew it was just nerves out of whack, but I felt overly tired. After putting on my pjs I decided to text Bobby.

I'm tired too. I think today took it out of everyone.

I think you're right.

Are you laying down?

Yes! Are you?

Yep. Wish you were snuggling up to me.

I giggled. **That would be nice.**

Hell yeah it would!

I laughed again. I knew he was just trying to cheer me up.

I love you, Katie. My heart fluttered.

I love you, too. I fell asleep with the phone in my hand.

Graduation morning went by in a haze. Everyone was everywhere at once. Mom seemed to be wherever I looked. She talked quickly and moved with insane speed. Her eyes held a hint of fear, but her face remained calm, and sweet.

My brother kept looking at me, but didn't talk. I wondered what he was thinking, probably about being able to take my room when I went to college. Gracelynn was bright and cheerful, which helped everyone's nerves I think.

Dad tried to keep busy with his newspaper, but tended to follow Mom around the house trying to be helpful. All the while, I sat and ate my chocolate puff cereal at the table, watching my family.

After breakfast, I started to get ready for the ceremony. I zipped up my dress and began to feel the milk curdling in my stomach as my nerves kicked into gear. Picking up the phone I texted Bobby with unsteady fingers.

Omg! I can't believe we're graduating! I hit send, and sent the same to Lane.

I know, right!? Eeeek! Cya there! I laughed at Lane's reply, wondering if she felt the same way. She sure didn't act like it.

I know babe, can't wait to see you. Bobby's reply made me smile.

Me neither. Are you nervous? I feel like I'm going to throw up!

Of course! He reassured me. **Kinda regretting pancakes!** I laughed quietly at his message.

Ouch! Yeah, I had a bowl of cereal and believe me….

LOL. I'll kiss you and we'll both feel better.

My heart did that silly little flutter at the thought of his lips.

Looking forward to that!

See you there, beautiful! Xoxo

K. xoxo back at you.

I put my phone down and looked at myself in the mirror. As I stood there, I thought about how different I felt. How different I looked. I never thought I'd be this girl. Boyfriend, a child to take care of, have a popular girl as a friend… I thought about Beth, and how much I really missed her. How she'd put my makeup on for me and do my hair. How we used to stay up late, watch movies, and talk about everything and nothing. I wiped a tear from my cheek and fixed my makeup. Grabbing the brush, I tackled my hair. My mom came in, her eyes instantly watering.

"You're so grown up." She walked up to me and I hugged her. It felt weird knowing that after this summer I'd be in a different place, finding my own way, living a whole new life. I hugged her a little tighter.

"You ready?" she asked.

I nodded, and she walked me downstairs.

"I have to stop at the office, but I'll be there in a quick few," Dad said, then after hugging me and Mom, he left.

We all made it to the school and I hugged my mom again before going in to get my cap and gown on.

Bobby was there, handsome in his black tuxedo. Lane was beside him in a beautiful, knee-length black dress. They both walked up to me, each of us smiling widely. Nervous and excited, we walked together. Bobby slipped on his gown, and Lane went to the bathroom to put hers on. I waited for them both before we took our seats.

The speech was typical, but I held back tears as they honored Elizabeth, showing photos of the whole class when we were young as well as a couple pictures of Beth. I missed her so much I thought my heart was literally breaking. Bobby squeezed my hand, and Lane held the other. I heard sniffles behind me, and then the speech was over. We began crossing the stage one by one as we'd practiced. When my name was called, I prayed I wouldn't fall on my face. I walked with my head high, and laughed as my family cheered loudly. I blushed when Bobby shouted "way to go, baby!" I shook the principal's hand, grabbed my diploma, and it was over.

Afterward, I had my picture taken too many times to count, and headed to the parking lot with my family. My dad hugged me, and handed me a set of keys.

There, front and center, sat a beautiful, glossy red Jeep. I felt my heart leap, and I jumped into his arms, before walking over to my new vehicle. My mom was crying, I'm pretty sure she hadn't stopped most of the day.

"You deserve it, baby!" she said, kissing my cheek. Then, she took a picture of me showing off my new ride.

I sat in it with Bobby, a little while later. We held hands and looked at the stars. "I love you." He whispered in my ear.

I snuggled into him. "I love you, too."

"It's going to be an amazing summer."

I nodded, and he pressed his lips to mine.

Later on that night I went through old pictures, and looked through all my yearbooks. I'd gotten a yearbook for every year at school. I remembered when I'd told Mom I didn't need them. She had told me that one day I'd want them. She was right. I looked at the photos, my eyes naturally finding Beth. Her eyes were bright, but her smile didn't quite reach them in most of the photos.

The next morning after breakfast, I got in my Jeep and went to the cemetery. It was a quiet morning. Warm. I took the letter out of my back pocket as I got closer. Then, I sat on my knees, not caring about the wet grass.

Beth,
Well, I graduated. It was just how I thought it would be...only, I barely held it together when they showed pictures of you. People that I thought didn't give a crap were even crying, and I guess in a way I feel good about that. They should care.
I miss you so much, every day... Every minute. You were my best friend, my sister, and even though you're gone... you'll always be my sister. You had an

amazing little girl, Beth, she's really wonderful. You'd love her, and you would have been an amazing mom. Every day I wish I could see your face. In a way I kind of do; Gracey looks so much like you! I find it hard sometimes to look at her. She has your eyes, and your smile. She's so beautiful, so smart. We all love and miss you Beth, I always will.

K&B 4 ever.

I folded the letter up, and put it beside the others that have become part of the soil.

"Do you come here every day?"

The voice behind me made me jump and I turned in surprise to see Beth's mom. "Sorry, you scared me." I cleared my throat and backed away a bit. "Not every day, but when I can."

She nodded, coming closer. For the first time, I didn't smell alcohol on her breath.

"She loved you," she said softly as she sat in the grass.

I kneeled beside her. "I loved her, too."

"I know…look.. I'm sorry." I raised an eyebrow.

"I'm sorry for not being a better mother to her every day. When she died… I guess it was kind of a wake-up call." I swallowed around a lump in my throat. "She would have wanted you to keep the baby. I'm glad you have her. Do you think it would be okay for me to meet her, though?"

I thought about that. I hadn't really been able to get a word in at all, but on the other hand, it was nice actually seeing that she cared and that she missed her daughter. It was about damn time.

"She looks just like her." I pulled out a picture of Gracelynn from my wallet and handed it to her.

"Oh my god!" she cried as she stared at the picture.

"I know… sometimes it's hard to look at her."

She began to hand the photo back to me but I pushed it toward her. "Keep it. I've got a million."

She nodded. "Thank you…Katie. You were a good friend. You were more family to her than I ever was. She was supposed to graduate today." She got up and walked away, studying the picture of Gracelynn I'd given her.

Wow! I guess people can really surprise you. I blew a kiss in the air, and with another look back I headed home.

CHAPTER 26

This Isn't The End, It's The Beginning

The heat was blistering but I didn't want to go. Bobby's hand caressed my stomach and he traced little circles along my hip. I closed my eyes against the sun and marveled at his touch. We were in our little spot, our favorite place. It was quiet, and I loved spending time with him here. This was our place. I wondered to myself if maybe it would always be our place. *Would it? Even after we were gone? Yes,* I decided. I smiled as his fingers tickled my waist and my eyes opened to see him looking at me.

"You are so beautiful." He leaned down to kiss me, his lips warm and inviting.

"We should probably go," I murmured against his mouth.

"You are probably right. I don't want you to burn."

I smiled up at him again. "Too late."

He took his time driving back to my house, we talked about how summer would be over before we knew it. Talked about my plans about Gracelynn. I had decided to take her with me after I got settled into the dorm and ready for her.

"I think you are very brave," he said as he stopped in the driveway.

"Or I'm crazy," I replied with a smile.

"Or you're crazy," he teased, as he leaned in to kiss me once more before he left.

I held Gracelynn's delicate hand in mine as I walked her to the swings. Her little legs were bouncing with each step she took. Ever since she'd started walking, it was non-stop go time. I pushed her lightly in the swing after buckling the safety belt.

"Weeee," she laughed.

Her laughter was a beautiful reminder of her mom. I watched her ebony curls bounce as she swung back.

"Momma!" she demanded when the swing slowed down too much.

"Okay Gracey," I laughed. I wasn't quite used to the momma thing, but the first time she'd said it my heart felt funny. I remember it kind of fluttered, then paused, then beat rapidly. I cried, both happy and sad.

I pushed my hair off my neck as the sun's heat beat down on me. I would have to get Gracelynn back home before long, it would be too hot soon. We'd discovered she didn't handle the heat well. It upset her stomach, and like Beth, she burned quickly. Her crying made me feel useless. I guess now I understood why my mom hated it when we were upset. It does something to a mom. I get that now.

"One more time, okay honey. It's getting hot."

Gracey looked at me. "Hot," she repeated.

"That's right, baby girl. " I gave a nice last push before I put her back in the stroller with the sunshade down. Before heading home

I gave her a drink of water. She loved drinking from my water bottle.

"Big girl," I encouraged her, earning a beautiful smile.

I took my time walking home, keeping as much sun off of Gracey as I could. Tonight was my last night of work. My boss was planning some sort of farewell, and a part of me wasn't looking forward to that. She'd cried when I put in my two weeks notice, admitting that she'd known it would happen. I had cried as well. Another chapter of my life is closing, and that scares the hell out of me.

That evening at the diner I was surprised. All my favorite regulars were there, and my boss had a chocolate cake made with 'Farewell Katie, We'll Miss You' written on it in purple icing. There were balloons, and some people brought presents. I hugged my boss.

"I really am going to miss having you here."

"I'll miss you, too."

She took my hand. "If you need a job next summer."

I laughed, "I'll be sure to check here first."

"You'd better," she nudged me.

Bobby picked me up from work and we sat together in our special place. His hand was warm in mine, his lips lifting every time he looked at me.

"I'm going to miss you," he said softly. He was going away to college to become a veterinarian.

I felt like crying "Hey, we'll figure it out," I told him with a smile.

"Are you sure you don't want to change your mind and apply, live with me…" his voice trailed away and I smiled sadly.

"I'm going to college here."

He leaned against me.

"I love you, Katie," he said in my ear, giving me goosebumps from head to toe.

"I love you, too. We'll call, and see each other whenever we can. We'll write, email. We'll make it work."

He nodded. "We will," he said, breaking the silence.

I glanced at the clock.

"Better get you back," he said as he glanced at me. He looked so sad.

"I can stay a bit longer." Before he could talk I put my arms around him and kissed him gently. His lips trembled against mine, and he drew me into him.

I don't know how long we sat there that way, lost in each other. When we pulled apart we were both gasping for air. Then, with a sigh, he drove me back so I could get my Jeep.

He followed me home to make sure I got there okay. As I walked up to the steps, I looked up to the stars. Tonight would be the last night before college. I went inside, and spent the rest of the night with my family.

A game of Monopoly, video games with Paul, a movie. When it was time for bed I tucked Gracelynn in her crib and moved a curl from her face. I sat with her until she fell asleep, and then joined my mom in the living room.

"You sure you want to stay in the dorm room and not here?" she asked me again. I nodded.

"I think it will be a good experience. Besides, we will see each other a lot. Gracey and I will need to come home to do laundry." Mom laughed. "I'm proud of you, sweetheart." She kissed my cheek and went to bed.

I took my time walking quietly through the house, turning off lights and smiling over memories. In my room I closed my door and studied the picture of Beth on my night stand. It seemed like so long ago, yet felt like only yesterday. It was funny how time did that. I put the photo down and climbed into bed. Sleep did not come easily.

The next morning I ate breakfast and finished packing the rest of what I was taking with me, and gathered up some of Gracey's things. The last thing I grabbed was the picture on my nightstand of Beth and me as kids. I stuffed the last box and suitcase in my Jeep and shut the door.

"That's it?" Mom asked, not bothering to hide her new tears.

I nodded, and walked toward her. "I'll be here in a week. To get Gracey, the rest of her things, and to do my laundry, of course."

Mom let out a sad laugh. "You be careful, okay?"

Gracelynn walked out holding my dad and Paul's hands. I hugged my dad and my little brother, and then lifted Gracelynn into my arms.

"Momma," she said happily. I smiled, trying not to allow myself to cry. I kissed her chubby cheek.

As I looked into Gracelynn's eyes I knew that life was forever changing.

Life is measured by every sweet moment, every imperfection. I hugged my family, and with one more look, I headed the only direction I could go.

Forward.

ACKNOWLEDGEMENTS

First, I want to thank my husband Michael for being by my side. Life with you has been such an incredible journey. Thank you for being my best friend. I am so grateful for your support, your patience, and for encouraging me throughout this literary process.

To my three amazing and beautiful children. You are my life, and without you, I wouldn't be who I am today. I want you to always follow your heart, You can do anything you set your mind to.

To my mom, for always being there for me, for loving me, and for cheering me on every step of the way. You are not only my mom, but my best friend. I love you so much!

I'd love to thank my extremely awesome editor, Valerie Irvine-Karinen. You have been amazing, thank you for all of your support, your feedback, your advice, and for your beautiful work! *Sweet Imperfections* has come such a long way because of your dedication and expertise.

I want to thank Abigail Gazda. You have been ever supportive, kind, and caring. You have made time for me and guided me. You have answered my questions and given me great advice and feedback. I appreciate you so much for your time, and your eagerness for my success!

Rhonda Lee, Thank you for your support. Your calls with Abigail have been so very helpful. You are such a kind-hearted soul, and I am honored to have the pleasure of knowing you.

I want to thank Susan Harring. It has been a pleasure working with you, thank you for such amazing work.

I want to thank a few very special friends. Thank you Lady Robin, Blythe, Krystal, Sara, Stacy, Diana. Your support and faith in my dreams has helped push me through some major self-doubt, and I love all of you so much. Many of my family and friends have stated "don't forget me when you become a bestseller and move away to be famous." I could never forget where I came from, nor my family and friends that have been by my side through this journey. I love you guys.

Last but certainly not least, I want to thank you: my readers. Thank you for having faith in this book; for picking it up and reading this story. Your support means the world to me. Books take us to a whole new world, they show us new experiences and connect us with different characters. I hope that this book was everything you needed it to be.

Thank you,
Love, Samantha.

www.ingramcontent.com/pod-product-compliance
Lightning Source LLC
Chambersburg PA
CBHW071427200726
48294CB00002B/544